Groundwood Books is grateful for the opportunity to share stories and make books on the Traditional Territory of many Nations, including the Anishinabeg, the Wendat and the Haudenosaunee. It is also the Treaty Lands of the Mississaugas of the Credit. In partnership with Indigenous writers, illustrators, editors and translators, we commit to publishing stories that reflect the experiences of Indigenous Peoples. For more about our work and values, visit us at groundwoodbooks.com.

Game Face

Game Face

Shari Green

Groundwood Books
House of Anansi Press
Toronto / Berkeley

Published in 2023 by Groundwood Books / House of Anansi Press
groundwoodbooks.com

We gratefully acknowledge for their financial support of our publishing program the Canada Council for the Arts, the Ontario Arts Council and the Government of Canada.

Canada Council **Conseil des Arts**
for the Arts **du Canada**

With the participation of the Government of Canada | Canadä
Avec la participation du gouvernement du Canada

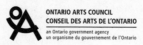

ONTARIO ARTS COUNCIL
CONSEIL DES ARTS DE L'ONTARIO
an Ontario government agency
un organisme du gouvernement de l'Ontario

Library and Archives Canada Cataloguing in Publication
Title: Game face / by Shari Green.
Names: Green, Shari, author.
Identifiers: Canadiana (print) 20220490325 | Canadiana (ebook) 20220490333 | ISBN 9781773068688 (softcover) | ISBN 9781773068695 (EPUB)
Classification: LCC PS8613.R4283 G36 2023 | DDC jC813/.6—dc23

Edited by Emma Sakamoto
Designed by Michael Solomon
Cover illustration by Julien Castanié

Printed and bound in Canada

Groundwood Books is a Global Certified Accessible™ (GCA by Benetech) publisher. An ebook version of this book that meets stringent accessibility standards is available to students and readers with print disabilities.

Groundwood Books is committed to protecting our natural environment. This book is made of material from well-managed FSC®-certified forests, recycled materials and other controlled sources.

MIX
Paper from
responsible sources
FSC **FSC® C016245**
www.fsc.org

for Nick

Pure

Neighborhood rink to myself
I lace up
my skates, brace
for the cold wind rushing
                around the corner.

I skate a few
laps to loosen up
        fly over bumps
and grooves
— nowhere near as smooth
        as indoor ice
but man, it's nice

no pressure from the clock
no spectators, no scouts
no parents shouting
        at the ref
        — and no ref
either.

No coach
no whistle
no stopping
        me now.

Others arrive
pick sides
            for a game.
I strap on my pads
head for the net
            and you can bet
I'm ready.

Skate blades scrape
stick bangs out a beat
            — he's open
picks up the pass
lines it up fast
            and shoots.

The puck echoes
            off the boards
— shot wide
            glove side.

I grin.

The icy wind blows
scatters snow
            like confetti.
My face stings, but my heart
            sings

cuz this

    is the closest thing I know

    to pure happiness.

Saturdays (Best Days)

The light fades, and I can't feel
my toes — head for home
can't wait
to thaw out
      warm up
             breathe in
the smell of Oma's cooking.

Dad and I aren't half bad
at making meals
but when Oma comes over
my taste buds start dancing
before I take a single
bite.

Tonight, Dad's favorite
hutspot — potato carrot onion
mashed together, topped
with thick slices of smoked sausage.

We heap our plates
carry them to the living room
settle in to watch
the game on TV.

Later, after Oma leaves
and we're washing dishes
          side by side
Dad asks his usual
Saturday-night question

          You got any homework, Jonah?

and I give my usual answer

          I'll do it tomorrow.

Then Dad nods
gives me one of his lopsided
          half smiles
as he hands me
a sudsy plate.
I dry it off
soak up
how *normal* this all seems
          how good and right
but I know the feeling won't last
so I tuck it away
to take out later
and savor.

Friends

I've known Tyrell Taylor
since our moms
taught us to skate
on the outdoor rink.
        I think
        we were three.
Been friends ever since
— always
got each other's backs.

I remember when I decided
        I wanted to play goal
Ty's eyebrows eased upward
like he was asking me
if I was sure
telling me to take time
be certain I was game
for the pressure
        considering everything
        that had happened.

I was.

I had to be.

Ty's the only one who knows

I used to throw up before
every game.
I don't anymore — it's all
under control. The past is

no
big
deal.

Now, Ty slides over
on the torn gray seat cushion.
I plop down as the bus lurches
forward, dragging us toward school
          ready
or not.

Racing

Group project in class
which probably seems
like a good plan
— it makes sense to share
ideas
      work
           skills
to come up with something
bigger
      and better
than I'd probably manage
on my own.

So why is my heart racing
before
we even begin?

Rose

The group work is for Monday
Poems. My heart quits hammering
when Mrs. Darroch lets us choose
our own group of three.
Maybe it won't be
so bad.

Noise erupts as kids call out
drag desks
            across the floor.
Ty and I share a quick look
            — partners
            without having to say it.
We glance around for a third
see Cole scooting
his chair in the opposite
direction.

I elbow Ty
jut my chin toward the girl
seated behind him
            observing
the chaos: Rosamie Garcia
my next-door neighbor.

Rose and her family moved in

a few years back
but she's only been riding our bus
since January, when her dad changed
jobs and couldn't drive her
to school anymore. Rose and I
don't talk much
               mostly because I'm always with Ty.
               She's nice, though, and I know
for a fact Ty doesn't mind
her perpetual humming
— a different song every day
               which is why some kids
               call her Jukebox.

Let's ask Rose, I say.

And just like that, she's part
of our group.

Ekphrasis

Each group must choose
a card printed with a famous work
of art. We pick a picture
of a ghostly man
hands slapped to his face
mouth painted in a big O.

We're meant to talk about
the artwork, share
our reactions, then each write
our own poem.

*He looks like Kevin
in the* Home Alone *movies*
says Ty
mimicking the gesture.

Rose says, *I like the sky
but it's strange
for a sunset — not exactly
peaceful.*

I don't say anything
because something
about the ghost-man
looks familiar

in a creepy sort of way.

As I stare at the picture
racking my brain for something
to say, the painted dark water
seems like it could rise up
and the ribbons of bold sky
could reach down, colors
swirling together, wrapping
around the man
pulling tight
— and it feels almost as if
they're tightening around me
right now.

I'm not about to put all that
in a poem
even though it seems
exactly the sort of thing
Mrs. Darroch said our poem
could be.

The Scream: Monday Poem by Jonah Vanderbeek

The ghost-man drifts toward home
on silent feet

stops dead halfway along the bridge
between there and here

remembers he was supposed to be
at a haunting.

Dilemma

Tuesday after school
it's warm
— barely below freezing
so I leave my coat open
don't bother
with my gloves.

When we hop off the bus
Ty's in a rush
to get home, grab his gear
head for the rink
before dinner
— he can't wait

but I
hesitate.

We've got a game tonight
I say. *And a math test*
tomorrow.

So what? Ty says. *We've only got*
a couple weeks left
on outdoor ice.

I don't want to care
about math
but if I don't do the practice
questions today
            tomorrow
I'll pay:
            sick stomach
            palms so sweaty
            I drop my pencil a dozen times
            before the test even begins.

I should study, I say.

You'll have time.

But what if I don't?
What if we lose track
            get back
too late
have to go straight
to the game? What then?

*Come on, Jonah. I need to
practice my wrist shot.*

*Your wrist shot's already
pretty good,* I tell him.

Pretty good? he says. *Pretty good
isn't getting us into the big league.
We've gotta be*
      exceptional — his fists
punch the air
      punctuate
pump up the intensity written
on his face.

I fidget with the zipper pull
of my jacket, run it
up   up
     down   down
don't say
a word.

Ty shakes his head
says, *Okay, I get it.
But tomorrow after school
I need you in goal. Deal?*

You bet, I say, forcing a smile
before turning toward home.

Somehow *not* going to the rink
ties up my insides
just as much
as if I'd gone.

How am I supposed
to focus on math
now?

Blur

Ty's psyched for the game
        even though
        I didn't play goal
        while he practiced after school.
He whips around the rink
in warm-ups
— a black-and-red blur
on a mission.

Coach waves us over.
Ty flies in fast
looks like he'll crash
into the boards, but he
sprays snow and stops
        like a pro.

He's breathing hard
when I arrive at his side
puts a hand on my arm
like he needs
        to steady himself.
I glance over.

Whoa, he says. *Head rush.*

He laughs, shakes it off
and his game face settles
into place
— no doubt
he'll get at least one goal
tonight. He claps me
on the shoulder
turns his attention
to Coach.

Game time.

Ready

I stand on the ice
        ten feet out from goal
staring, gaze inching
up one red post
        along the crossbar
                down the opposite post
sending a message
vowing to do my part
        if the posts do theirs.

Finally I skate into the crease
rough up the ice just enough
scrape my blades
        side
to side
        until it's perfect
then park myself in net
settle into position
ready

        except

        for the acrobatics going on
        in my stomach
        and the *what-ifs* rattling
        a doorknob in my brain, threatening

to burst in and ruin
everything.

Time to Think

I play best against the Bears
because they're tough to beat.
All their forward lines
        skate fast
        pass well
        shoot hard
and even Thomas and Harjit
— our strongest D — have a tough
time breaking up their plays
which means
I face a ton of shots
don't have time to listen
to the *what-if*s in my head.

If only
we were playing the Bears
tonight.

Instead it's the Wildcats
bottom of the league
poor guys hardly ever win
a game. The puck
is always in their end
f o r e v e r
so every period is another twenty minutes
for me to think:

What if the Wildcats' passing
suddenly clicks?

What if they changed up their lines
and a guy they never thought could score
has an incredible shot?

What if every shot he takes
goes in?

Knots tangle together
tighten
in my stomach.

What if the Wildcats trounce us
and I'm the guy
to blame?

      DING!

A puck rings
off the left post
       coming out of nowhere.

My heart
                    ricochets
          inside

                                        me

a pinball
          striking every nerve.

HOW did I not see that?

I suck in a deep breath
give the post a tap
with my stick
thanking it
for saving my bacon
but Coach bellows —

VANDERBEEK! PAY ATTENTION!

at which point the knots
in my gut
cinch up

way
too
tight.

Spew Haiku

Oma's meatball soup
looks disgusting when it's spewed
all over the ice.

Benched

Ty's mom meets me
by the washroom door
eyebrows pinched together
worrying
over me as if I'm her own
kid. She asks twice
if I'm okay, offers
to drive me home.
I tell her
it was just something I ate
tell her my stomach
       has always been
       a bit fussy.

I should know better, I say.
*Shouldn't eat so close
to game time.*

I return to the bench
discover the on-ice cleanup
       complete
and Kyle, our backup goalie,
       in net.
Coach pats me on the back
tells me to take it easy

says Kyle will handle it
from here.

I'm fine, I tell him. *Really.*
Because even though
          everyone
saw what happened
and part of me
wants to get out of here
          ditch
          the rest of the game
a bigger part of me
needs to get back in goal
show them
          it was nothing.

Coach points
to the empty spot
next to the defensemen
— Kyle's usual place
on the bench.

Apparently
barfing
          equals
                    benched.

Dreams, After

One warm day
the first summer After,
half a dozen of us
were playing road hockey
like we did more days
than not.

An impatient driver
in a pickup truck
       who must've forgotten
          or never known
       how perfect it feels to
       play for the Stanley Cup
       (even if it's not
       for real)
blared his horn
when we didn't move off the road
fast enough to suit him.

Once his path was clear
he stomped on the gas
peeled away
while we carried the net
back into place.

I'd barely settled into position
when my dad came barreling
out of the house, wild look
on his face.

You could've been killed! That's it.
This is way too dangerous.
Find something safe
to do.

I couldn't look at the guys, stared
at the asphalt instead, wishing
I'd sink right through it
and disappear.

Dad's words were directed at me
but they broke the spell
for everyone. Suddenly the game
was no fun, the sun was too hot
                for hockey.

Dad went back inside, muttering
about idiot drivers, and my friends
took their sticks and wandered
away.

Ty hung around long enough
to help carry the net

up my driveway.

I stayed out in the garage
a long while, cross-legged
on the cool concrete floor
the image of my dad's
panicked face running
through my mind.

I knew things could go wrong
— things had already gone
horribly, terribly wrong
in our lives
but I still wanted
to play.

Sure, I worried some
but I wore pads and a mask
and I listened
for cars. It wasn't enough
for Dad, would never be enough
to keep him from stressing out.

What if someday I got
as bad as my dad?
What if I became the one
squashing the fun
out of every single thing

all because of what *might*
go wrong?

I couldn't let that happen.

I was different from Dad
and I knew exactly
what it would take
to prove it.

When the next hockey season
rolled around,
there was no backing down.

I was a goalie
and I was going after my dream
no matter what.

Mystery

I've never been sure
I did the right thing
choosing
to play in goal.

Will it prove
I've got what it takes
to go after my dreams

or will it prove
I don't?

Morning Routine

Anything? Dad asks
pouring himself a large mug
of decaf coffee.

I skim the headlines for him
same as every morning:

politics?
       nothing earth-shaking
       for a change

natural disasters?
       some serious earth-shaking
       out on the west coast
       (but Dad doesn't need to know that
       or we'll be moving to Saskatchewan
       this afternoon)

crime?
       definitely nothing
       he should hear about

entertainment?

The new Marvel movie is out.

He nods
sips
and I close the news app
set my phone aside
and finish my cereal.

When I got home from
last night's game
I didn't mention
my great meatball-soup mishap
because Dad
would read into it
make it
a big deal
and the last thing I need
is a big deal.
So I told him the part
where we won 8-3
and left it at that.

Are you going to the parents'
meeting tonight? I ask him now
knowing the answer already.
Even before the accident
Dad didn't go to meetings
if he could manage
to get out of them.
Oma will be there, he says.

Okay. I just wondered.
You know — in case they talk about
anything important.

She'll be there.

I finish getting ready for school
grab my backpack and gloves
pause
before heading outside.

Are you working at the office
today? I ask.

Unfortunately, he says with
a grimace. Dad hates tax season
hauling himself out of the house
to see clients
more days than not.

Me and Ty are going
to the rink after school
okay?

He's going to remind me
to take my helmet.
            W a i t for it ...

Ty and I, Dad says. *That's fine, just
be careful. And wear your helmet.*

I fight to keep
my eyes from rolling.

As if
I'd forget my helmet.

As if
I'd risk taking a puck
to the head.

Rose stands at the bus stop
blowing out puffs of air
      like little clouds
        that drift for a moment
           then vanish.
Down the block, Ty's racing
the bus to our stop.

What's new with you? Rose says.

Not one single thing.

No Comment

Rose claims the first open spot
and I move to the back, plunk down
stow my backpack under my seat
as Ty lands in the space beside me.

We rehash last night's game
run the play-by-play
for each of his three goals
— a hat trick's sweet
even against the Wildcats.

We analyze the defense and dissect
the few saves I had to make, hockey
commentators broadcasting
from the back of a yellow school bus.

We don't comment on the one thing
begging for attention. Instead
Ty gives me a nudge that means
don't worry about it.

Coach shouldn't have benched you
he says without looking at me.
Thanks, I tell him, even though
we both know he's lying.

Enforcers

Dylan Babinsky and his buddies
barrel around the corner
like on-ice enforcers searching
for a fight, ready to drop their gloves.

The guy on Dylan's right
is on my team — Bennett. He's bigger
than Dylan, but not as mean
           not usually, anyway.

Hey, Jonah, Dylan hollers
over the buzz of hallway chatter.
I don't look at him
           pretend I didn't hear
fumble as I spin the combo
on my locker.

The crowd thins out
clamor fades
as kids vanish
into classrooms.

I'm talking to you, Vanderbeek
Dylan says. *Or maybe I should call you
Vander-barf.*

Heat rises
          in my face
as his friends crack up.
I look over my shoulder, shoot
an evil eye at Bennett. Of course
he told Dylan
about me barfing.

Ugh.

If I hadn't left my pack on the bus
gone back, made myself
almost late
I wouldn't be dealing with Dylan
alone.

I slam my locker, hope
to reach homeroom
                    before Dylan

                              reaches me.

When I turn
          he's right there
leering
and I'm racking my brain
for a witty comeback
          — humor's good
                    in these situations, right?

but then his expression
            twists
and loud retching noises
burst out of him
            mocking
            mimicking.
The other guy joins in
fake-barfing in my direction
until all of them
            Bennett included
break into hysterics, laughing
all the way to class.

Yeah.
Hilarious.

Hide

Three lates mean detention
which means missing the bus
walking home

because Dad doesn't drive
        not since the accident.

I dash
into class
as the second bell sounds
slide into my seat
beside Ty.

Some days I wish
I had an invisibility cloak
so I could hide
for a while
from bullies
        and barf jokes
from my dad's worries
        and my own
from late slips
and mistakes
and being
me.

When I look up
Mrs. Darroch smiles.
Good to see you, Jonah.

Simplify

Next class is math. Ms. Krieger
hands out the test — two pages
of simplifying fractions.
I know this stuff
had no problem
with the practice questions
but as a test paper lands
on my desk
I'm pretty sure I've forgotten
everything I ever learned.

I glance around the room
            as if my brain power
            might be floating nearby
discover Dylan watching me
from the back row.
He sticks a finger
in his open mouth
mimics a silent gag.

Why does he have to be
in almost *all* my classes?

I turn away
clutch my pencil
knuckles whitening
chest tightening.

Improper
            proper
numerators
            denominators
numbers swimming
on the page. How am I
supposed to simplify
these fractions
when my brain wants
to magnify
my reactions?

Pencils scratch
            pause
scratch again
as people around me
work out their answers.
The sound burrows
into my brain
brings numbers back
into focus
loosens the band
            around my chest.

One number
        one question
                one answer
at a time
my mind totally
(ten-tenths, one hundred-
hundredths) focused
so there's no room
for other thoughts.

I got this.

Some Days, Out of the Blue

Lunch bell rings, I swing
my bag over one shoulder, ride
the tide flowing
toward the cafeteria, surrounded

by jostling, joking, sound
and movement filling
every inch of the hall. Unheard
above the chaos, alarm bells

clang in my mind, eyes dart
search for escape, a break
in the current. I slip
into the space between
a closed door
and a bank of lockers
breathe
        breathe
                breathe
dive in again, until

the crowd pours
through double doors, disperses
among long tables. I find
my usual spot with the usual
group, paste on a grin

pull out my sandwich
and carry on as if
I didn't just survive

a tsunami.

Big League

It snowed last night — not much
but enough that the rink
will need clearing.
It's three-quarters done
when we get there
thanks to Mr. Garvin.
He must be eighty years old
— skating along, slow as can be
pushing the rink shovel

                              down to the far end

and back

                              down

and back.

Says he likes the exercise
but I think he does it
just to be nice.

Ty grabs another rink shovel
zips along on his skates
finishing the job
while Mr. Garvin takes a break
leans against the boards
mops his forehead with the back
of his gloved hand.

More kids arrive
   Cole and Harjit from my team
   Curtis from down the block
   Rose and her little brother
and we get a decent game going.

Eventually it's just me
and Ty again
one on one.

The outdoor rink transforms
into an NHL arena
Ty with a breakaway
wicked wrist shot
   — he scores!
Again and again
slapshots
backhanders
more wrist shots
   he's good
   but so am I
glove save
stick save
bounce-off-my-helmet save

  Sorry, Jonah!

and we play until our stomachs
scream that we're late
for dinner.

Just you wait, says Ty
as we unlace our skates.
When we get drafted
to the big league, it's gonna be
spectacular. Imagine
playing hockey
for a living! Doing this
— he gestures at the rink
every day of our lives.

Imagine.

Yeah, I love this.

If it's like this, it'll be
amazing.

Plans

Ty has birthday money he's itching
to spend on a new stick
so Saturday afternoon
we hop a ride on the city bus
get off at the sports store
go inside and drool
over the store's collection
of signed NHL jerseys.

As Ty finally gets down
to picking a stick
my phone buzzes with a text
from Dad.

> Running errands with Oma, then
> she's taking me to the theater.

Oma's been working on him
for weeks, saying they both need
a night out — but I know
she goes out by herself
all the time
now that she's retired
            (Spanish lessons
            dance class
            book club)

so this is about getting Dad
out for a change.

cool
what movie?

A play at the fancy dinner theater
downtown. Got your house key?

I text him a thumbs-up.

There's pizza in the freezer.

My phone will be on silent. I'll
check it, but if there's an
emergency call the theater.

Right.
Like I'd ever call
and ask theater staff
to track down my dad.

I want to tell him there's never yet
been an emergency
when he's left me home alone
but that would probably lead to him
        listing all the potential disasters
        he can think of

which would probably lead to me
          wondering whether any of them
          are legit possibilities, so …

have fun!

Ty's heading to the cashier
          stick in hand
so I tuck my phone
in my pocket
don't bother reminding Dad
about my game tonight.
What he doesn't know
won't stress him out
— might as well let him enjoy
the play.

My "Don't-Worry" Note for Dad

Dad,
Game
tonight.
Got my gear
and water bottle.
Ty's mom will drive me home after.
Last game before playoffs! Don't worry — I'll be careful.

~~Don't Worry~~

I shouldn't have said
don't worry — it'll only make him worry
more. But seriously

does that always
have to be my
problem? Maybe I'll beat
him home tonight, but if not
he'll just have to deal.

> I hope
> he can deal.

I rummage through my hockey bag
tap each piece of equipment
picture myself head to toe

mask
to
skates.

If I'm missing any of my gear
if anything fell out
> on the garage floor
I'll end up on the bench
and Kyle will get to start

in net. That's no way to impress
no way to make my mark
no way to prove I've got
            what it takes.

When I'm sure it's all there
I zip the bag
slip the cord with my house key
around my neck
tuck it beneath my shirt
and hurry outside to wait
for my ride.

If they forget to pick me up
            I'm sunk.

If they pick me up
but then run out of gas
            I'm sunk.

If they pick me up, have enough gas
get there on time, but I'm missing
a piece of equipment
            I'm sunk.

I crouch beside my bag
unzip
scrounge for each piece
one more time
               just in case.

Ziiiip.

As I straighten up
Mrs. Taylor's SUV
pulls into my driveway.

Weird

We're two and two against the Bears
this season. Tonight's game decides
who we're up against
in the playoffs
so there's a lot riding on it.

Ty looks over at me
as his mom pulls into
a parking space.

We need this win, he says.
You got this, right?

Why is he saying this
        now
           right before we hit the dressing room
                right when I'm starting to regret
           the microwave pizza
           I scarfed down for dinner?

Yeah, I got this. Geez, Ty.
It's the Bears. I like playing
the Bears.

We climb out of the car
wrestle hockey bags and sticks

from the back and head inside.
Mrs. Taylor wishes us good luck
disappears in the direction
of the bleachers
and Ty and I haul our gear
to the dressing room.
We drop our bags, claim
the space beside Cole.

Ty inspects the tape-job
on his new stick
then glances around
lowers his voice.

Kyle's not good against
the Bears, he says.

Seriously? Ty thinks I'm going
to play so lousy
Coach pulls me and puts Kyle
in net?

I yank my jersey
over my head.

I'm not gonna hurl mid-game
if that's what you're thinking.

(I'd better not.
Oh, man, what if I do?
If it happens again
Dylan will *never* let me
live it down.)

I know, he says. *Sorry.*
It's just that I heard
the coach of the rep team
will be here, checking us out.
We've got to look sharp.

He doesn't say it, but I know
he's thinking
all our dreams rest
on tonight's game
which makes no
sense, but I'm sure
he's thinking it.

Shut up, Ty.

What? I'm just sayin'.

Weird — it's not like Ty
to up the stakes
not like him
to doubt me

at least, not to my face.

Maybe he's always doubted.
Maybe he thinks I'll never
      be in control.

Maybe he thinks
        I'm like my dad.

              Maybe
              he's right.

Hand-Me-Downs

Some things are perfect for passing
down from father

       to son

like the collection of worn
Roald Dahl paperbacks
from when he was a kid

or his super-soft baseball mitt
that I love
       even though I don't really care
       about baseball

or his famous *words of wisdom*
and the stories about Before
       (because I really don't want
          to forget Before)

but the one thing I hope he *didn't*
       pass down
is the one awful thing I hate
about him.

Pressure

Second period
the Bears pile on the pressure
fire shot after shot.
Ty nabs the puck, passes, but
it deflects off a skate ...

No!

No Chance

Scramble

    leg shoots out

        s t r e t c h e s for the pad save

                no chance

                too fast.

                It's in.

Misconduct

The goal light flashes on
crowd groans
our players
        deflate.

I whip around
see the puck
tucked in the corner

— disbelief

even though I know
it's a goal.

Ty
        in my face
so close. His eyes blaze
but his voice
is ice — *I thought you said
you had this.*

I did have it, I say
jaw tightening, heart
thumping. *You're the one
who blew it.*

He mutters something, turns away
while every one of my anxious fears
and stressed-out doubts race
to escape, shoot through my body
         up
shoulders, arms, hands gripping
my stick

           and I swing

slash the goalpost

                         stick bounces back

whirl
around, frustrations flying
hard and fast
      slash
the air —

          I see it
          before it happens

                    but it's too late.

My stick strikes
the leg of a Bears player. He goes down
his teammate shoves me

Ty shoves
him, all of us
pushing, tangling
gloves dropping
fighting.

The officials pull us apart. Equipment
litters the ice.

In our zero-tolerance
league, we all know what's coming:

we're out of the game.

Doused

A good fight can light
a fire under a team, but
our bench is quiet, flames
doused by a wave
of reality:

our star forward
and our starting goalie
just got themselves thrown
out of the game.

Eternity

Ty slams the gate behind him
causing it to bounce back
unlatched. He doesn't break stride.

By the time
I get past Kyle, who's moving in
           to take my place
Ty's already stormed his way
through the tunnel
— I'm slower
thanks to my goalie pads
slower still
because I catch the look
on Coach's face.
He says something to Rob
the assistant coach, juts his chin
in my direction.

I turn away
take a left
toward the dressing room.
The two guys from the Bears
have already vanished
down the hall to the right.

Ahead of me, a mound of gear

lies on the floor
at the dressing room door

stick   gloves
skates   helmet

only it's not just gear
it's Ty.

Trip over your new stick? I say
sneering, still mad
about his lousy pass
        my failed save
madder now that I'll miss
the rest of the game.

I catch up to the Ty-pile blocking
the door, slap his leg with my stick.

Move, I say
but he doesn't

not

        at

                all.

Two things

happen at once:
a voice shouting behind me
      — Rob
and a kick to my gut
      as I'm hit
            with the sure fact
            Ty isn't faking.

I bend over
drop my gear
nudge Ty's shoulder
and silently beg him
to jerk awake and laugh
      in my face
            — *gotcha!*
but Rob rushes in
knocks me aside
      so I fall on my butt
      in the narrow hallway.
Rob glances up
as I struggle to my feet.
I half-expect him to say sorry
for the bump

and *hey — what's with Ty?*
but instead there's a glare
      a look that says
      what have you done?

I want to tell him it wasn't me
but no words come out
can't say anything
in my defense
because maybe it *was*
        my fault.

        It was me
who let in the goal.
        It was me
who swung the stick and started
the fight.

I step back
lean against the wall
might still fall, so I sink
to a crouch, Rob hollering
for help.

Ty

on his back now
Rob bent over him
watching his chest
        is he breathing —
        he must be
        got to be
        how could he not be breathing?

People in the hall
feet pounding toward us
Rob's hands pushing on Ty's chest
    hard
            again
            again
            again
frantic voices
        more people.

Someone wrestles with Ty's jersey
scissors slice through fabric
Velcro rips, shoulder pads shoved
out of the way
Rob barely breaking rhythm
pumping on Ty's chest
again again again.

A woman
        red rec-center shirt
slaps two pads on Ty's
bare brown chest
wires, an automated voice
      shock advised

then Rob
voice strong but threaded through
with panic —

Stand clear, he says
and he stops pushing
on Ty's chest
sits back on his heels
hands up, not touching

      Ty

and the machine zaps
      shock delivered.
In a flash Red Shirt's hands
are on Ty's chest
taking over for Rob
and WHAT IS HAPPENING?
      TELL ME
WHAT'S
GOING
ON.

Nightmare
straight off a TV drama
but there's no camera
and Ty is no actor.

He's my best friend.

Air

Paramedics — two of them
   and a gurney
crowd into the narrow hallway

so narrow
   is it shrinking?

A fight, I hear Rob tell them
then *I don't know*
he was down
unresponsive.

His words are far away
like I'm hearing them underwater
like I'm sinking
   drowning
   where is the air?
Ty's not breathing and now I
am not breathing
can't breathe

   why is there no oxygen?

Need to find a place to breathe a place
   with space
   to fill my lungs. I crash

against the bar on the exit door
stumble outside
find myself in the parking lot
        behind the arena
cool night air washing over me
hands on thighs, bent over
like I just ran sprints
gasping until breath
starts finding its way in

without a struggle.
I look across the parking lot
        quiet
        everyone else still inside
weave my way between
frost-covered cars
to the sidewalk.

Pause.

Look down.
        My skates — I'm still wearing
my skates.

The blades will be toast.

Going Home (and Not Going Home)

I tuck my goalie pads
under one arm
and head for home, skates clutched
in the opposite hand, fingers growing numb
against the blades, laces
              dragging
                            on the ground.

Cold seeps from the sidewalk
through my socks
slows
        my
                steps.
My boots
coat
bag
still in the dressing room
rest of my gear on the floor
        in the hallway

the hallway
where Ty …

I glance over my shoulder
squeeze eyes shut
        for a moment
then keep walking.

It's dark
— no moon
only isolated pools
of light from streetlamps
glaring down on the mounded
snow beside driveways.

I finally reach my house
        lights on, door not locked
        Dad must
                be home.

I stumble down the hall
close myself in my room and strip off
the rest of my gear
kick it
beneath the bed.
I pull on pajama pants, dig
through a drawer for warm socks
layer them on and climb under
        my quilt.
My heart beats superfast.

Dad knocks.
You're home early, he says
through the door. *I didn't hear
Mrs. Taylor's car.*

Right. She was going to drive me.

It's not like she would've
looked for me, though
not like she had a moment
to wonder if I found a way home
not when Ty
wasn't even going home
        at all.
She'll be at the hospital with Ty
probably rode in the ambulance
with the two paramedics
and Ty on the gurney
racing
to the emergency room.

Are they still pushing on his chest?
Still zapping his heart?
Is   he   okay?

My door opens and Dad
peers around
checking on me. *How was the —*
His expression freezes. *Jonah?*
What's wrong?

For a moment, Dad white-knuckles
the doorframe, then rushes
to my bedside.

He launches into his routine — scans me
          for blood
          broken bones
presses his palm against my forehead
          checking for fever
gets in my space
studies my face
and finally
                    breathes.

I'm fine, I say, even though
I'm the opposite
of fine.

ICU

It's Ty, I tell Dad. *He's hurt
      or sick.
         I don't know.*
*The ambulance came
to the game.*

Dad closes his eyes
for a second, shakes his head
the slightest bit
and I know he's thinking
he *knew* something like this
would happen
knew it was only a matter of time
before Ty or me or some other kid
      got injured
only a matter of time
until it all
      went

            wrong

and now I know
he was right.

Dad goes to his office to call
the closest hospital. I follow.

Tyrell Taylor, he says into the phone.

I hover while he waits
stay close so I can hear
even though I'd rather shrink back
       hide escape pretend
        this isn't happening.
Dad finally gets some information
and hangs up.

Is he okay? I ask.

They figure he was rerouted
to the children's hospital.
I expect they're better equipped
to care for him there.

Another call
another wait
another wish
       to disappear.

The hospital won't tell Dad anything
but he finally gets through
to Rob   listens   hangs up
rubs his hands
over the stubble on his face.

I'm sure you want to go see him
Dad says
> but I'm not at all sure
> don't know
> if I want to know
> if I want to see
> if I can handle
>> any of this.

Dad continues, *But he's not really*
aware or awake. We can't
visit yet, anyway. Family only
in the ICU.

ICU?

Dad nods. *Intensive Care Unit.*
When it's something serious
when someone needs
> *extra care*
that's the unit
they're put in.

Serious.
Intensive.
Extra care.

Ty might've taken a punch
during the fray, but the Bears' forwards
were no enforcers. And Ty — he's tough
            bigger than I am
there's no way
they could've done major
damage. Could they? It was only
a little fight.

But there was nothing else.

Just my slash
            retaliation
penalties

and then Ty
            on the ground

an ambulance
the Intensive Care Unit
and a cold weight
            moving through me
limbs growing heavy
muscle and bone replaced
with solid blocks
of ice.

Evidence

A noise outside
          and a knock on the front door
and my stomach flip-flops like
a fish on dry ground, shaking
my legs awake. I hurry
to the door, imagining news
about Ty. No one's there
but my hockey bag sits
on the cold step, goalie stick
lying across it, glaring
at me.

I wish it had busted.
Snapped in two, or
been lost, or stolen.
But here it is, making sure
I don't forget
what I did.

I look up, see
a pickup parked in front of our house
engine still running and Cole's dad
standing beside it, hand
on the door handle, looking back at me.
He waves, then gets in and
drives away.

Text Regret

Back in my room
I pick up my phone
tap on his name to send a text
he won't get — not until
he wakes up.

Whenever that will be.

how are you?

What a thing to
ask a guy in the ICU.

I send another text
try to say what I mean.

I hope you're okay

Better.
Not enough.

Could any text be enough
to tell Ty I'd give anything
everything
to fix this
to erase the fight

if it's my fault
and even
if it's not.

Third time's the charm
right?

I'm sorry

Just put down
the phone, Jonah.

Tossing & Turning

I'm tired
so tired but my mind
won't shut off, won't leave
me alone so I can sleep, keeps
firing messages that hit me
like cross-checks.

What if Ty's not okay?

        What if he doesn't
get better?

What if he gets better but
letting in that goal ruined
everything so Ty
will never get picked
for the rep team, his dream
is destroyed, our friendship
is over
        because of me?

Who'll be my partner
for group projects
and play Xbox hockey
with me and keep
my secret?

Who'll take my big-league
hopes and dreams as seriously as I do
even if becoming a goalie
was the most ridiculous
thing I ever decided
to do and if I'd never done it
my best friend would be okay now?

      But I did, and now Ty's
not okay and might never be
okay again.

Next Morning

When the doorbell rings
I can't bring myself to open
my eyes — hide under
my covers, ignore the light
shining through the crack
in my curtains because it can't possibly
be morning.

I barely slept, never did manage
to quiet my mind. It was like
a tiny alien creature invaded
my brain, took over
the controls. Even though
I tried telling myself
everything would be fine
the alien kept sending his own
it's-not-fine messages
practically all
        night
                long.

The bell rings again.

I drag myself out of bed
step into the hallway
        and into the sound

of Dad's snoring coming
from his room
pull on a sweatshirt
as I go.

A whoosh of cold air hits
my bare toes
as I swing open the front door
find Rose standing there
— Rose, from next door
  Rose, from school
    Rose, who has never before
    set foot on my front steps.

What are you doing here? I say
which I admit isn't the most polite
way to greet someone
but give me a break
— I just woke up after one of the worst
nights of my life.

Good morning to you, too, she says.
I brought you some toast.

She extends a plate
stacked high.

Um ... why?

I heard about Ty, she says. *I figured*
you'd be upset. My mom
always takes cassava cake
when people are upset.
        She shrugs
        with one shoulder.
I didn't think
you'd want cake
for breakfast. Therefore

toast.

Two years ago, after the accident
all sorts of people came by with food
— meals I didn't have any
appetite for — but Mrs. Garcia
brought cassava cake.

Mostly the only thing I remember
from those first days
was the way
my dad got up each morning
made coffee
said thank you to people
who came by
        the whole time looking
        like he wanted to scream.

But I also remember
cassava cake.

Cake would've been all right, I say.

Triangle

Rose stands there with the plate
        waits
so I take it. She doesn't leave.

You want to come in?

Thank you, she says
pulling off her boots and trailing
behind me to the kitchen.
Do you have any jam?

We climb onto stools
sit at the island
eat triangles of toast
with raspberry jam
don't say much of anything
at all. It's weird
        but also maybe a little nice.

After a while I get up
pour two glasses of orange juice
pass one to Rose.

She thanks me, then says
I understand, you know.
I figure she's talking about

my best friend
being stuck in hospital
and me being stuck wondering
if I'm the reason he's in there
            and how can she possibly
understand that?

I take a big swig
then swirl the OJ in my glass
watch it climb up the sides
like it wants to

                                        escape.

This juice gets it.
This juice understands me
better than Rose ever could.

Rose brushes crumbs from her hands
hops off the stool
sets our dishes
            in the sink.

I should probably say something
            at least thank her
            for the toast
but a heavy door closes
inside me. Before I can free

any words, Rose says
I hope he's okay.

And then she's gone.

Should've Been

My phone dings
with an incoming text.
I grab it off the couch
— a response to the pathetic
messages I sent Ty
last night.

I'm hit with a wave
of *thank goodness*
       of *I'm so glad you're alright*
          of *holy hospitals, Batman*
          you had me freaked out.
But a second later
the wave rushes back
to wherever it came from
leaving me cold
       and wrung out
because the text
is not from Ty.

hey, it's Lewis

Ty's still in the ICU

Lewis is Ty's brother.
He's fifteen

and never talks to me and Ty
when we're over there
playing NHL on the Xbox.

My thumbs tap out a question
— *Is he ok?*
Don't hit send
backspace
erase
stare
at the blank spot waiting
for my response.
If he's in the ICU it's clear
he's not okay
                not yet.

Is he going to be ok?
Delete delete delete.
If the answer is no
I don't want to ask the question.

how is he?

awake but pretty out of it

After another minute
of staring at my phone
I text again.

thanks

for replying, I mean

no prob

saw your message when I got
here this morning. one of the guys
on your team dropped off Ty's
phone and jacket and stuff

not that he needs any of it right now

One of the guys.

Should've been me.
I should've been there
should've looked after Ty's things
should've gone to the hospital even though
I wouldn't have been able
to see him.

Should've.

Didn't.

What kind of friend am I?

Monday

Rose stands
on my doorstep
again.

No toast today? I ask
meaning to tease
but it comes out dull
as if my voice has no energy
          just like the rest of me.

I could make some, she says.
If you want.

I was kidding.

So was I.

A smile twitches at one corner
of my mouth
disappears
before it turns into anything.

I was just wondering
if you're going to school, Rose says.
I could pick up your work for you
if you're not.

Last thing I feel like doing
is facing everyone at school
but Dad insisted I go
said routine
was important, said getting
behind in class
wouldn't be any help to Ty.

You wouldn't go, I told him
last night, *if it was you.*

> You
> who landed your best friend
> in the Intensive Care Unit.

> You
> who wrecked
> everything.

It's true — he wouldn't go
if it were him.

Don't turn this on me, Dad said.

You're going to school.

This is going to be
the worst Monday
of my life.

Bubble

Rose sits beside me on the bus
in the spot I normally share
        with Ty.
She hums a song that's vaguely
familiar.

Not many kids from
our homeroom ride
this bus, but I'm still surprised
nobody asks
about Ty. Coach emailed
all the team parents yesterday
— said Ty was awake
but still in the ICU
        which I already knew
        from Lewis.
You'd think the news
would've traveled
faster than Connor McDavid
on a breakaway

but maybe not.
Maybe no one outside our team
has heard.

But then how …

Rose, I say, and she stops
humming and looks at me.
How'd you know about Ty?

Cole's parents go to the same
church as my mom. They were
at Mass on Saturday night
when Cole phoned to get picked up
after they ended the game
early. Mom said their phone rang
right in the middle
of the Our Father.

Cole and Bennett are the only
other guys from the team
who are in our homeroom.
Maybe they've told everyone
and there won't be any questions
after all. Maybe I'll be able
to slip into class
                    unnoticed.

The bus arrives at school
door opens, and we all step outside
join the river
of students flowing
toward the main entrance.

Rose dodges around a kid
crouched in the middle of the hall
tying his shoe.

As she again falls into step
beside me, the same familiar tune
fills the space between us.
And still, no one presses in
with questions about Ty
        about the fight
                about what really
                happened.
Not a single person stops me
to dig for details.
It's as if Rose's humming
has wrapped us both
in a bubble of calm
        and quiet.

The moment
we walk into Mrs. Darroch's room
the bubble
        bursts.

Swarm

The kids in my class
swarm around me — bees hungry
for some sweet gossip.

Spin

Is he okay? I heard he's in a coma. Did his heart really stop? Did they really have to shock him? Is it true you knocked him out in the dressing room? I thought you guys were friends …

Game Face

Mrs. Darroch's voice
        breaks in
kids drift away
        take their seats
and the buzz
                fades.

I glance at Cole on the other side
of the class, wish for a moment
they'd surround *him* instead
ask *him* instead. But Cole doesn't know
the whole story.

        He didn't find Ty
on the floor, didn't see Rob
        working on him, didn't feel
the walls closing in
        the air
                vanishing.

I sink into my chair
stare at my desk.
        My eyes sting.
I blink, try to pull myself
        together

need
to get out of here.

I raise my hand
lift my chin
catch Mrs. Darroch's attention.
     Bathroom.
I only mouth the word
but she understands
and nods at me.

I slip out of the room
make my way
to the boys' washroom.
It's deserted.

     Deep breath in
and out
     peer into the mirror
pale skin now flushed pink
press fists against my eyes
until they quit leaking
bend forward over the sink
and rinse my face
     with cold water.

I grab a paper towel
look again

at my reflection
ready to paste on
my game face

my *I got this* face
my *everything is fine* face

before heading back to class.

Instead, I freak out
for half a second
when I think I see
my dad's eyes
looking back at me.

Monday Poem: Two Voices

Mrs. Darroch asks us to pair up
for today's poetry project.
Rose and I both end up
      odd ones out
so we find ourselves working
together. I'm glad to partner
with her, because truth is
I could use another dose
of calm.

We start with a Venn diagram
like we use in math
— overlapping circles
to illustrate what Rose and I
have in common.

She suggests our topic
should be *families*, but I
veto that, not keen
on something that's bound
to turn serious or sad.

*How about hobbies
or sports we like?* she says
but I toss out that idea too

because sports
will lead to hockey
      and hockey
            will lead to Ty.
Already, there may as well be
a giant spotlight
over Ty's empty seat.
The space
where he should be
draws my attention
      a powerful magnet
pulling my thoughts
from our two-voice poem
to the fact that my best friend
is lying
in a hospital bed.

Rose brings my attention back
to our task, and we finally
focus on *food*
— Filipino favorites
I've never heard of
and Oma's specialties
which are foreign to Rose.

The middle is easy
— a list of things
we both love:

                pizza
                peaches
                Cheetos
                cassava cake
(which Rose has loved
                forever, and I've loved
                since the day her mom
                first baked some for
                my dad and me
                        After).

I wonder what we'd find
in the overlapping middle if
we made a Venn diagram
about our families.
I almost wish
I hadn't rejected that idea.

We write separately
about our differences
then create the part about
similarities together.

Our poem grows from
her words
                my words
                        our words

like two voices
singing different parts of the same song.

Favorite Foods: Monday Poems by Rosamie Garcia and Jonah Vanderbeek

Rose:

Just when I decide I can live
on nothing but pizza, Mom
fries up a batch of lumpia.

Suddenly I'd trade all the pizza
in the world to see Lola
in the kitchen with Mom again

moving around each other
in harmony, cooking and dancing
to the tune of family.

Jonah:

To keep my strength for hockey
I have to eat a lot.
While any food will do it,
Oma's always hits the spot.
Her cooking seems to make me think
I've really got a shot,
like she adds a cup of courage
stirred into the pot.

Rose and Jonah:

cassava cake tastes
like sweet milky coconut
and making a friend

Off My Game

Practice tonight
but it doesn't seem right
to play
       without Ty
— I struggle with my gear
stumble
       stepping onto the ice
let in the weakest shots
and fall on my butt
       twice.

Dreams, Before

When hockey season started
the year I was ten
we were finally allowed
to pick positions

            specialize
and even though I played in goal
for fun on the outdoor rink
even though being an NHL goalie
was my absolute
        ultimate
           dream
when it came time to
choose, the thought
of being the last line of defense
mobilized a thousand
butterflies in my stomach.

I had to search for my voice
when the coach pointed
at me, waiting
for my top choice.

I knew what I wanted
to say
        wished I could say
but what finally came out

was all wrong.

Defense, I said.

The butterflies froze
as if the whole of my insides
had been petrified.

I still played in goal whenever
we hit the outdoor rink
still studied techniques
of the pros

                    and still dreamed
it might
       some day
be me.

Parachute

hey, it's Lewis

hey

this is so messed up

my little brother in the ICU

yeah, scary

I'm glad you were there

when it happened, I
mean, so he wasn't alone

Guilt rises up
e x p a n d s
            wraps
around
to smother me.

I force it down, shift my focus
to Lewis. It's not like him
to talk to me. Must be

he's freaked out, worried
about Ty.

I flash back to the day Oma met me
at school, the moment I knew
something terrible had happened, but
I didn't yet know what.

When Lewis got called
to the hospital, I bet
it felt a little like that — like the earth
had dropped away.

There's an instant filled
with a million questions, an instant
before you plummet
into another world.

And then you

fall.

I hand Lewis a parachute
of empty words:

Ty's tough. He'll be okay

Beat

Dad calls my name
late that evening
when I'm getting ready for bed.
I find him at his desk
in the den, still surrounded
by what he calls *organized chaos*

papers stacked
          everywhere
computer screen on
phone in hand
pencil
          behind his ear.

He indicates the phone
— *Got another email*
about Ty, he says.
From your coach.

I don't breathe.
Search
Dad's face

— good news?

          bad?

He stares at the screen
scrolls
reading
  or rereading
and I want to yell at him
to hurry up
tell me
what it says.

He nods to himself
and finally
explains.

Turns out
there was something wrong
with Ty's heart
long before that night
at the rink.

Hypertrophic cardio-
  Dad hesitates
between syllables, checks the email
again
  -myopathy. It means
his heart muscle
grew too thick in some spots
made it tough to keep

the beat, keep the blood
        pumping
        the way it should.
They figure Saturday night
it couldn't beat right
went a little wild

        and stopped

until that shock
        — pads and wires
        on Ty's chest
got the beat back.

On Wednesday
he's having surgery
to put a miniature version
of the shock machine
right inside him
        under his skin
with a wire to his heart
to zap it
if it ever loses the beat
again.

Then he gets to come home.

That's great news, Dad says
and I nod.

But is it?
What exactly
does it all mean?

Will he be ... My voice
fades, the words
melting
into cold questions
in my head.

Will he be the same Ty
as before? Will *we* be the same?
Or has everything
changed?

It wasn't me
wasn't the fight
wasn't anyone's fault
            at all
and yet
I still feel like the ref
is pointing at me
glaring
giving me
            the boot.

Texts for Breakfast

I texted Ty late
last night, and this morning
there's still no reply. I fire off
another message
while I wait for my toast
to pop up.

you allowed visitors yet?

yeah, but don't bother
I'll be home on Thursday

it's no prob — Oma
can drive me

...

...

...

I'll just see you after I'm home, k?

The toaster flings my breakfast
right onto the counter.

I leave it
where it lands
head back to my room
to get ready for school.

Strangers

I trail behind Oma
wait while she talks to the man
at the reception desk.
Already my gut's telling me
it's a bad idea to surprise Ty
when it seems he doesn't want
to see me. But we've been friends
forever — he must not
have meant it, probably
he was just tired.
I won't stay long.
Only long enough
to see that he's really okay
and tell him in person
            I'm sorry
            I let in that goal
sorry about the slash
and the fight
it started

            — if he'll listen.
            If he doesn't yell at me
            to get lost, go home, never
            come see him again.

Stop dragging your feet, Jonah
Oma says, *or we'll never get there.*

Up the elevator
along a bright bare corridor
left turn
right turn
through a maze
            of strange smells.
Oma slows
examines room numbers
stops by an open door.

Inside, Ty's sitting in the bed
book open on his lap. His mom
dozes in a chair beside him.

Oma taps on the door frame
and Ty looks up. He grins
but the smile falls away fast
like he suddenly remembered
he was mad at me.

Mrs. Taylor wakes up
and before I know it
she and Oma go in search
of coffee and I'm left

standing awkwardly
next to Ty's bed.

We say *hey* and not much else
       as if we're strangers.

Listen, I finally say. *I'm really sorry.*

Me, too, he says, and hope
rises. Maybe he and I
are okay.

So, I say. *You getting that thing
put in your chest?*

*A defibrillator. Yeah.
Tomorrow.*

Cool.

His eyes flash
       a shot of anger
and just like that
Ty steals away my hope
— a quick poke-check
the moment I dared
let down my defenses.

He turns his head
toward the window.

After a few moments
his shoulders rise and fall
in a heavy sigh.

I can't play hockey, he says.

It's just playoffs left anyway
I say. *Only a couple games.*
And you'll be good as new
in time for next season.

No, he says, still
not looking at me. *I mean*
I can't play hockey

> *ever*
> *again.*

Robbed

When a goalie makes an unlikely save
takes away what seemed to be
a sure-thing goal for the other team
they say the goalie robbed
the shooter.

Unlikely saves and sure-thing goals
seem like specks
        single snowflakes
        in a blizzard
when I think of all that's been taken

                                   from Ty.

No more contact sports.
No "intense activity."
No more big-league dream.

Man Down

After dinner
Dad turns on the game.
I swallow my guilt
try to bury the idea
that I shouldn't even *watch* hockey
the night before my best friend
has surgery
— my best friend
who will never race
        around the rink again
never zip past the defense
        on a breakaway
never score with his
        wicked wrist shot
        again.

It'd be wrong
to enjoy this game
too much.

I grab a notebook and pen
from my backpack
sit on the living room floor
        legs stretched out
        under the coffee table
half-heartedly focus

on homework
while the other half of my heart
tries not to pay too much
attention to the game.

Second period, a player goes down
after a brutal check
       — a penalty for sure.
He doesn't get up.
I quit pretending
to do science homework
gaze now glued
to the TV as the guy's teammates
signal for the trainer.

The trainer hurries out to help
       skittering
across the ice.
Players from both teams
gather
wait
probably holding
their breath like me, wondering
if he's going to be okay.

I asked my dad once
why he watched hockey on TV
but could never bring himself

to come see me play.

I love hockey, he said.
I just don't love the idea of
everyone firing hard black missiles
directly at my son.

Now, memories snake
around my chest
squeeze hard as the seconds
tick by
— Ty down
          unresponsive
paramedics rushing to his side
with a gurney.

Sure, with Ty
it was his heart
— not exactly due
to hockey
          not really.
But next time somebody goes down
it could be all hockey's fault
          a knee injury
                    a concussion
                              a bad cut
                                        from a skate.

It could be me
or Cole
or anyone else
on the team — if the pros
can't avoid getting hurt
what hope
do any of *us* have?

I swear, if they have to
bring out a stretcher
for this guy, I'm never setting foot
on the ice again.

Stars

Our playoffs will be knockout style
— one loss and you're out.
Since the league agreed
to call our last
unfinished game
a tie, we're set to play the Stars
on Friday night. It should be
an easy win
cuz to be honest
not many of those Stars shine.

Next game we'll be against
the winner of Kings
versus Wildcats
— like it's any mystery
who'll survive that match-up.
Kings have crushed
the Wildcats all season.

We'll have a decent shot
at beating the Kings
and if we win
we'll play
for the championship

but why am I the one

who gets to play? How *can* I
when Ty has been permanently
benched? I don't even know
if I can play without him

or if I want to

      or if he'll hate me
      if I do.

I get ready for bed
cross to my window
gaze out at the clear night sky and wish
upon every star up there
that the playoffs
get cancelled.

Teeth

Mrs. Darroch gives her usual
Wednesday morning book talk
but even her enthusiasm
for the hardcover
she's hugging
can't keep the alien
in my brain from stealing

my attention. Pesky thoughts
sink their teeth
      into my mind
no way I can shake them off.
Ty's in surgery this morning
maybe this very minute. What if
something goes wrong?
And if it all goes right
      (it *has* to go right)
but he hates me
if I play hockey
           can't stand to be with me
           even if I give it up
will we ever
be friends again?

I shouldn't play — I won't
      I definitely won't

because of Ty
but also because of injuries.
         Dad was right
it's crazy to stand in goal
while the other team pummels me
with pucks.

I wonder
         how Ty's doing
                  right now.
Is it over?
Is he awake?
Is he in pain?

Argh!
Shut up, brain. Pay
attention. He's fine — I'm sure
he's fine, and it's not like
I can change anything
anyway
by thinking the same thoughts
a million times.

The class has moved on
to Book Share time
and a hum of voices hovers
in the room as kids talk up
their favorite books

with their friends.
I tune in to Rose and Alexis
but next thing I know

      Ty
      hockey
      Ty
      surgery

an annoying song playing
on repeat
over and over
the volume
cranking up a notch
every time
until the noise in my head
drowns out Rose
and Mrs. Darroch and the entire
eighth-grade English class
and inside, I'm shouting
at the alien, screaming
over the racket
for it to please

    SHUT UP!

A sudden silence

not within
but around me — the classroom
has gone quiet.

I hollered out loud?
I slouch lower in my chair
feel my face flame.

Everything okay? Mrs. Darroch asks.

Yeah, I mutter. *Sorry.*

A girl across the room
giggles, and everyone relaxes.
Mrs. Darroch passes around
large index cards
for book recommendations
to post in the school library.
Rose watches me for a moment
then turns to the cards
spread over her desk.
She hums as she works.

A harsh whisper from Julianna
who sits nearby — she turns
her head just enough to glare
at Rose, hurls words
over her shoulder:

Knock it off, Jukebox.

Compared to my outburst
you wouldn't think a bit of music
would be a bother.

Rose stops humming
bows over her work, pencil flying.
When she's done, she slides
a card onto my desk — a cartoon
with two frames

       a jukebox with eyes
       and a sharp-toothed mouth
       a stick figure saying *Shut it, Jukebox*

       the sharp-toothed mouth
       devouring
       the tiny stick figure — *munch! crunch!*

I stifle my laughter
dig in my bag for a red pen
mark a bold A+
but even as I'm grinning
       enjoying
       the joke

inside I'm a cave
      empty
      and dark.

I pass the *munch crunch*
stick-figure comic
back to Rose.

If only it was as simple
to demolish
my alien.

No Signal

When a player suffers
a sprained knee
a bruised shoulder
      or a heart
        that stops beating
people can see he's down
and they know
      help is needed
they know
      to signal for the trainer.

Right now, waiting
      and worrying
while Ty's in surgery
it feels like the alien
hit me hard from behind
and I'm down on the ice
hoping someone
will signal for help.

The trainer doesn't come.
Play doesn't stop.

Don't they know
      I'm not okay?

jello

We're outside at lunch break
and everyone's avoiding
me, because hey
if you yell *shut up* at your own thoughts
what do you expect?
I don't have the energy
to talk to them anyway, and besides
I'm on a mission.

I slip around a corner
to the quiet side of the building
slide down, back against brick.
The cold seeps in.

I pull out my phone, hope
for a message from Ty
but there's nothing.
I tap on his name, thumbs
hovering, want to ask
if he's okay, but if I do
            and he doesn't text back
what does that mean?

No possible answer makes me feel
any better, so I finally send
a hand-wave emoji, wait

with my insides tangled up
and my heart in my throat
— nearly drop the phone
when it pings.

> all done – easy peasy
> eating yellow jello

A strangled laugh bursts from me
and my eyes go from dry to pouring
in the time it takes
for me to text back
a high five.

Flood

When Rose finds me
I'm still bawling, even though
I should feel better
not worse.
It's like everything inside me
has been squeezed tight
for so long, the pressure
is forcing out gallons of tears
which, come to think of it,
is not all that different from
when I get so wound up
I barf. Tears are tidier
but you can't write them off
as the flu or a fussy stomach.

I swipe my sleeve
across my eyes. My face
is dry for about two seconds
before the leaking resumes.

Ugh.

Rose sits beside me on
the freezing concrete
and doesn't say a word.

The bell rings
          time for class
but there's no way.

Come on, says Rose.
You should go home.

She leads me in through
a side entrance, past shop classes
and down a hallway filled
with kids at lockers — sixth graders
who won't dare mock
a hockey-player-sized eighth grader
          (who by now
has become a giant
snot machine).

When we reach the main office
I gulp in a couple
stuttering breaths
don't meet the secretary's eye
because it's one thing to cry
like a baby, and quite another
to let others witness it.
I mumble something
about needing to go
home.

Are you sick, dear?
asks the secretary.

Not exactly.

Rose jumps in.
Yes, she says. *Can't you see?*
He needs to go home.

Why don't you go wash your face
the secretary says to me, *and then*
you can tell me what happened.

What happened, Rose says
is that he needs to go home.

Thank you, Rose. Jonah looks like
he'll be just fine
given a little time.

Just because you can't
see a problem
doesn't mean he's fine.

Rose — the secretary inhales
a deep breath
blows it out slowly —
you need to get to class.

Rose turns to me, says
It's social studies and math
this afternoon. I'll copy
my notes for you.

The secretary calls Mrs. Darroch
who says of course
I can go home
because she knows
what a wreck I've been.

I ask for permission
to use my cell, call Oma
to please pick me up
then I slink to the row
of orange padded chairs
to wait.

Haiku at Oma's House

Oma's ginger cat
leaps onto my lap and purrs.
I breathe easier.

*

Should I tell Oma
about my alien thoughts?
I don't think I can.

*

The cat nudges me
and I whisper my secret
into her soft fur.

Clobbered

After Dad's done with
his last client of the day
Oma and I pick him up
and drive to our house.
I disappear
        down the hall
leave my bedroom door open
just enough for words
to slip through.

Oma's voice, low
        and serious:

*You need to talk
to him, Greg. He was in
tears at school.*

Did Mrs. Darroch tell her?
        Did the secretary
                or Rose?
Or was the evidence
still etched on my face
when she arrived
to get me?

*Ty being in hospital
has us both
stressed,* Dad says.
I'm sure he's fine.

He's not fine.

*You don't think I can tell
whether or not my own son
is okay?*

No, I don't!

There's a pause
and when Oma speaks again
her voice is calm.

*I've seen you struggle
seen you get better
did my best to support you
when you abandoned treatment
after Melanie died.*

My mom's name
jabs my heart
          a quick jolt
and Dad's next words
float past

without pausing
in my ears.

I recover just in time
to be clobbered
by Oma's reply.

He's just like you.

Shatter

I jerk back
shove the door
don't care
that it slams

drop
          onto my bed
whole body hollow
as Oma's words
echo
          in my head.

Breathe fast
up again
pace the room
          she's wrong —

I went to school
even though my brain
begged me to stay home

visited Ty in hospital
when my gut
would've been happier not to

played in goal

game after game
faced shot after shot
all season long

all of which my dad
would
            not
                    do.

I grab my pillow
muffle the growl
that erupts
from my throat.

It's NOT TRUE.

Thoughts from somewhere
            deep
in my brain

wriggle their way
            to the surface

— weight on my chest
knots in my stomach

running running running

when kids at school swarmed
when Ty needed me
when Mom

                    died.

An invisible force
tries to crush me
now.

My stomach threatens
to spew my lunch
now.

My legs itch
twitch
like they want to run
now.

I fling the pillow from me
let it fly across the room.
It steamrolls my desk lamp
knocks it to the floor

        ceramic base
        busts in half

        bulb
        shatters.

A Piece of the Story

The crash and clatter
satisfies something inside
as if breaking the lamp
broke my anger, and I'm left
with an empty, sick sensation
in my belly.

Dad comes into my room
glances at the pillow
near the wreckage
on my floor. He picks up
the two halves of lamp
from among the shards of bulb
cradles the broken pieces
in his hands.

*I'll get the broom
in a minute,* he says
not even asking
about the lamp.

He stands there a moment
not saying anything
then pulls out the desk chair
with his foot, sits with the lamp
pieces held on his lap.

I perch on the edge
of my bed, pull up a corner
of the quilt, twist the fabric
around my fingers.

Finally Dad clears his throat
says, *You know how I am.*
How I don't drive
don't go out much
— that sort of thing.
> *Do you know why*
> *I'm like that?*

I shrug, not sure I want
to look him in the eye.

Because of worries? I say
making it sound like a question
even though I know
it's the truth.

Sort of, he says
and I look up.

Sort of
means there's more to it
than worries.

Sort of
means I only know a piece
of the story.

The Truth about My Dad

Even when I was little
Dad wasn't a fan
of meetings or events
but he would go out every weekday
to work at the office.
Since the accident
he mostly works at home.
I thought it was so he could be here
to take care of me
now that Mom
       wasn't
didn't realize it wasn't a choice
didn't realize he couldn't manage
going out to his job anymore.

He used to drive
when we went somewhere
       the three of us
       together.
He never replaced the car
after the accident
and I didn't clue in for ages
that not driving was not at all
about having no car
and one hundred percent
about an awful mix

of worries and sadness
not letting him get back
in the driver's seat.

He never did go to my games.

When I was little
I pretended I didn't mind
that he seemed to care
more about work
than me and my activities
            but I *did* mind — still do
            if I'm being honest
but at least I know now
it isn't because he doesn't care
enough, but that he cares
            too much
worries too much
can't stand to watch
or even
barely
think about it.

The truth is
Dad's worries existed
Before
but got much worse
            After.

The Truth about Me

I catch a glimpse of myself
in my dad's nervous face
nearly every
single
day.

Control

Dad fusses with the lamp pieces
restacks them
on his lap.
Finally he twists around
in the chair, sets the broken
bits on my desk
then faces me again
             back straight.

Everyone has worries
from time to time, he says.
But for me, it's more than that.
I have an anxiety disorder
— a kind of illness.
I'm trying to get better
or
             I was trying.

He hesitates.

I wrap the edge of the quilt
around one hand
             unwrap
wrap again.

But I'm not here
to talk about me, he says.
Oma wonders
and I wonder
if you might be struggling
with the same kind of thing.

I freeze
fabric clenched
in my fists.

I go out, I say. *I play hockey.*
And I'm going to drive
— when I'm old enough.
I will.

He shifts in his seat
sighs heavily
as if talking about this
takes every speck
of his energy.

It isn't really about driving
or not driving, he says. *Anxiety*
is more about worries
and scary thoughts being
out of control, getting in the way
of living life.

I'm sure there are things
you worry about, he says.
But your worries
— they're not
out of control

                        are they?

His face is a familiar tangle
of love and fear and his voice
practically pleads for everything
to be okay.

I let go of the quilt
smooth the fabric beside me
lift my chin
and tell him exactly
what he needs to hear.

I'm fine.

Clarity

In the dark
Dad's words sink
into my heart.

Truth drifts
across my mind
barely there

takes shape
becomes solid
settles into place.

The alien
          in my brain
has a name.

Part of me
wants to ignore
the problem

bury the evidence
keep it hidden
in shadows

but maybe
it would be easier
if I brought it

into the light.

My Old Pal, Al

Dear Alien in my Brain,

We both know your real name
is Anxiety, but I'm not ready
to introduce you to anyone else.
Still, we should be on a first-name
basis by now, and Alien doesn't
quite seem to fit. Can I call you Al?

~~Your friend,~~
~~Your enemy,~~
Your host,

Jonah

Clouds

Dad has to go out after lunch
to see clients. He reminds me
      like he always does
that his cell number
office number
Oma's number
are on the index card
stuck to the fridge
      like they always are.

Is he going to treat me
like a kid forever? I bite back
my reply, let him have this
bogus bit of control
over potential disaster.
He shrugs into his jacket
and steps outside.

I watch him start
down the sidewalk
almost wishing I'd gone
to school today, almost wishing
I didn't have the afternoon
stretching out ahead of me
      empty
but Dad and I both figured

I needed a home day.

He wants me to rest
think about what he said
yesterday. So far I haven't managed
to think about anything else.

Dad waves
at an oncoming car
— the Taylors' SUV.

Ty's on his way home
from the hospital.

They drive past our house
disappear around the curve
in our road.

I pick up a book
            put it down
flick on the TV
but don't watch, wander
through the house.

He'd want to see me
right? Might be wondering
what's taking me so long
to get to his house.

That day at the hospital
— he wasn't himself.
His text
          yesterday
seemed more like the Ty
I know, more like nothing
has changed.

I should go.

I cross the street
walk a block
knock
          on Ty's front door.
Mrs. Taylor answers
ushers me inside with her
usual welcoming smile.

Her hand settles
on my shoulder
and her expression
morphs
          lips press together
          brows pinch
and she says,
          soft, so it's just
          between us

Maybe don't mention hockey
okay? It's going to take time
for Ty to adjust.

I go up to Ty's room
say hey, ask if he's feeling
okay.

He sits on the floor
with a bin of Lego bricks
keeps searching through
         yellow black red blue
rummaging
for the perfect piece
while the thing we *don't* talk about
hangs in the room
like dark clouds scowling
before a storm.

Rescue

By the time I leave Ty's place
the awkwardness in the room
has grown thick enough
to smother us both.

I breathe in cool air outside
squint at the pale sun
plod the long block
back home.

A short while later
the doorbell rings
and I hope for a second it's Ty
come to dust off our friendship
and start again

       but it's Rose.
I guess school's out
for the day.

I brought your homework
she says. *I can go over it*
with you, if you want.

We sit in the kitchen
books and papers spread

across the table.
I tell her Ty's back home
and she tells me about Julianna
giving Dylan what for
for hassling a sixth grader
between classes.
Then we get to work.

Rose hums a song
I don't recognize.
The notes
                    float
        in my head
and for a moment I forget
about my math worksheet.

Why do you hum all the time?

Immediately I wish
I could pull the words back
inside me.
            Was that rude?
            Is Rose going to be
            upset?

Can't help it, she says without
glancing up from her notebook.

Whew.

I mean, it sounds nice
I say. I just wonder, is all.

Rose gives me an odd look
like she's sizing me up
deciding
how serious I am.

My lola — my grandmother — she loves
music. She used to dance me around
her living room when I was small
used to sing all the time.
Even after her mind got sick
and she forgot so many things
she still remembered
the songs.

When my grandfather died
last year, Lola had to move
to a care home. Now she wakes up
in a place that's strange
to her. She looks for my grandfather
but he's not there. She looks
for the home she remembers
but she never finds it.
It scares her.

She pauses, and there's a
fierceness in her eyes
like she's daring me
to call her grandmother foolish
for being afraid, but I just
swallow down thoughts
of my own fears and wait
for Rose to go on.

Every morning before school
she says, *I call the care home*
get Lola on the phone
and I sing with her.
It helps her not be afraid.

I imagine Rose with a phone
to her ear, rescuing
her grandmother with music.
          I wonder if Oma
will need rescuing someday.
What then? She's the one
who's always rescuing us.

The quiet gets uncomfortable
so I pull my thoughts back
to right now, grin at Rose.
And once you start singing
you just can't stop?

She smiles back
lifts one shoulder
in a half shrug.

I guess when you start your day
singing away
someone else's fears
your heart can't help but hang
on to the song.

Reprieve

Is it really true?
"… refrigeration problem.
Playoffs are postponed."

I read the email again.
Yes! Two weeks for rink repairs.

Spring

Friday morning at school
Cole and Bennett complain
about the delay of the playoffs.
Two weeks of the arena
being closed for repairs
seems like eternity to them.

We can't even skate
on the outdoor rink, Cole says.
How are we supposed
to stay sharp?

He's right
about the outdoor ice.
Spring sun that's almost
warm has left it slushy
mushy, full of ruts.
We're not allowed on it.
If things were normal
Ty would sneak out there
when it froze over every night
and skate anyway.

But not me — no doubt
I'd catch an edge
wipe out
wreck my knee.

So that's it
no more hockey
for a while.
I force my face
into a grimace
that I hope doesn't look
as fake as it feels.

Yeah, I say to Cole.
What a drag.
My shoulders sag

but as I head to my desk
I can't hide the spring
in my step.

Wish

I
dream
one day
time will be
miraculously
reversed so things can spiral back
to a day of pure happiness on the rink with Ty.

Almost Perfect

Dad and I have one of those
perfect Saturday afternoons, except
this time there's no hockey first

no one-on-one with Ty
no teams patched together
for a never-ending game
goofing around
with half a dozen pucks coming
at me at once, and all of us
laughing
faces frozen
by the winter wind

so maybe it's not even
close to perfect
but still, it's a good day
> Monopoly and Uno with Dad
> then Oma coming over
> take-out pizza
> a movie

> and not a single mention
> of anxiety.

I don't think about Al
until late at night
house silent
and me lying in the dark
with zero chance
of sleep.

Rowdy

No hockey means
no worries about
equipment
missing an easy save
getting injured
losing my dinner
       on-ice

no stress to impress
coaches, teammates
or myself

no need to prove
anything.

I felt lighter today
less tangled up
but now in the dark
       the pressing-in dark
the space in my brain
that opened up, calmed down
like a crowded
classroom emptying
after the bell — that space
       vanishes
as other thoughts

rush in, rowdy and rude
jockeying
for the best seat:

        the playoffs will still happen
don't let the team down
        how can I be so happy
        about no hockey
when Ty would give anything
to play — seriously, what kind of friend
am I

                    and are we even
                    friends anymore
        I better not dare think about
        playing even when the rink reopens
        because how could I
just face it, whether I play
or don't play it's going to be
the wrong decision
        I'm going to ruin
        everything, disappoint
        everyone, and probably
                    flip out and run away because
everyone knows I can't handle
the pressure so
                why
        do I even

                try?

I roll over in bed
face down, pillow
over my head
as if that might block out
the roar of my thoughts.

Hope Is a Ping

My phone pings
— a text

    from Ty.

                                                           `hey`

                         `wanna come over?`

`yes!`

An exclamation point?
Seriously?
Dang, that was too enthusiastic.
Now he's going to think
I'm too hyper, too weird
too something
probably going to change
his mind.

                                                            `cool`

I take my time
tying my shoes
        making up

for the exclamation mark
then   s t r o l l
speed up
        catch myself
        and slow   down
walk

to Ty's house.

Pieces

Lego pieces carpet
the living room floor
around Ty. I skate through them
on my sock feet, clearing
a path before claiming
a spot near the couch.

Whoa, I say
surveying the projects
he's already built
— a gray-and-green castle
      for tiny Lego wizards
an almost-all-black
      pickup truck
a multicolor stairway climbing
      to the coffee table.

You've been doing
a lot *of Lego*
since you got home.

I'm so bored, he says.
But I'm supposed to
      take it easy.

He scans the remaining

pieces. *See any more wheels?*
I'm making a trailer.

I help him look.
I want to ask how he feels
but somehow it seems
like a dumb question.
He *looks* fine
but he can't be fine
        — is he fine?
He seems more like
himself than on the day
he came home — at least
he's talking to me. Maybe
he was just tired then.
Of course he was, but
is he okay now? I should ask
but words …

       hello, words — where
       are you when I need you?

Finally I blurt out
a tiny piece
of all the things
I want to say.

Does it hurt?

He glances up from fishing
for bricks. *Kind of,* he says
going back
to the Lego. *But mostly
my chest is sore from Rob
beating on it.*

The arena …

Ty's voice seems to go a bit
                distant
while images
of that night drift
behind my eyes
                a slideshow
I've scrolled through
way too many times.

*The doctor said I'm lucky
I don't have broken ribs.
I guess — well, you saw — Rob
was pushing on my chest
pretty hard.*

He nabs an axle
snaps it
onto the trailer.

But at least it worked
he says. *Or the zap did.*
I don't remember much
from that night.

His expression scrunches up
like he's searching his mind
for missing pieces
of the puzzle.

When did I even wake up?

I … I'm not sure.

I must've been awake
when they put me
in the ambulance.
I remember seeing my mom.
Her face — oh, man
she looked
       freaked out.

He shakes his head
like he's shaking out
the memory.
Then he grins.

Sirens and lights, though

he says. *Pretty awesome
right?*

I must've been halfway home
by then. Were the lights
flashing, siren
blaring as the ambulance sped
from the arena?

Maybe.
I don't know.

I wasn't there.

The Whole Story

My insides wrap themselves
into a tight ball
        tighter

            ~~tighter~~
and Al fires messages at me

        get out get out get out

I deflect them
kick them   off
        in

                all
directions
        can't keep this up much
        longer
force myself to click
a few more bricks
into place
then make my excuse

                        and leave.

My mind's no quieter
at home. I've never hidden
things from Ty — he knows

how my thoughts and worries
mess me up. He knows
the truth …

just
not about this.

How can I not tell him
the truth?

I pull out my phone
send him a text
          before I can decide
          it's a bad idea.

I wasn't there

where?

that night — when you woke up

I'm sorry. I didn't mean to run

you left?

you mean after I was in the ambulance?

before that

after my mom got there?

before

...

after they revived me?

A huge lump forms
in my throat
and my thumbs tap out words
I could never say.

I meant to stay

I don't know what happened

What happened is
I freaked out.

What happened is
my anxiety took control.

What happened is
I deserted my best friend.

I'm sorry

I give up waiting
give up
          hoping

abandon
my phone.

Debate

I should've told him in person.
    I should've kept the truth to myself.

I should've gone to the hospital sooner.
    I should've given him more time.

I should've shut out the alien thoughts.
    I should've found a way to breathe
    in spite of them.

I should've stayed.

    If only
    I'd been able
    to stay.

Monday Poem: Acrostic

We're supposed to write
an acrostic poem
about something that matters
to us. Rose's arm shoots up.

Can it be about anything?

Mrs. Darroch nods.

Whatever's on your mind.

Before I even know I've decided
what to write
my pencil marks the letters
in bold capitals
lined up like a tower.
After that, it isn't hard
to complete phrases for each letter.

> **A**lien in my brain
> **N**ever leaves me alone
> e**X**tremely annoying
> **I** wish it would go
> **E**xit
> **T**ake off and never come back
> **Y** … WH**Y** CAN'T I MAKE IT STOP?

I tear out the page
ball it up
shove it into my open pack
by my feet.

I should write about Ty
or hockey
but instead
I drum my pencil
on a fresh sheet of paper
          waiting
for my imagination
to settle down and focus
on something
safe.

Secret Spilled

On the bus home, Rose holds out
a very wrinkled sheet
of notebook paper
— my stupid
not-meant-for-anyone-to-see
poem. I snatch it
from her hand, shove it
in my coat pocket
snarl at Rose.

You took this?

She huffs out a breath
and shoots me a look.

Of course not, she says.
*But burying things
doesn't always keep them
hidden. It fell out
of your backpack. You really
should zip it closed, you know.*

I always close it. I was distracted
is all. Distracted by Al.

You figured it was fair game
then? Thought you'd help yourself?

Better me than, say,
Dylan Babinsky.

Huh?

Dylan was reaching for it.
You were already halfway
to the door.

Oh, I say.
Well
thanks.

Did she read it? Is she thinking
I'm weird or weak or
messed up? And dang —
thank goodness Dylan
didn't get his hands on it.

I stare out the bus window
as we rumble past brown lawns
          peeking through the remains
          of the snow.
Even if she didn't
read it on purpose

she couldn't help but see
the bold black tower
spelling out my secret.

You want to tell me
about it? she says
as casual as if
she's asking the score
of a random hockey game.

No!

Okay. But it seems like
it takes up a lot of room
in your head.

She shrugs one shoulder
up
        down
in a very *Rose* gesture.

Sometimes talking about
a problem
shrinks it a little, she says
so it doesn't take up
so much space
inside.

Possibility

I can't imagine words
shrinking my
worries
down
to

n
o
t
h
i
n
g

like sunshine
and a warm wind
melting away the snow

but

last week Oma said Dad
abandoned treatment
which must mean

        there's treatment.

Medication, maybe
but I wonder

if talking
is treatment
too

if words
might be a warm wind
for my worries.

Time Out

The idea of asking
for help — signaling
for the trainer
            telling another person
what goes on
in my head
puts Al on high alert, thoughts coming
too fast and now I'm breathing
too fast have to slow down
slow
            down

        s l o w

            d o w n.

Time out, Al.

If *thinking*
about talking
            telling
                        asking for help
makes everything
worse
there's no way *actually talking*
will work.

Top Five Reasons *Not* to Signal for the Trainer

1. I'll probably panic.

2. Everyone will know I'm hurting.

3. More fuel for Dylan Babinsky!

4. Dad will get even worse
   when he finds out I'm *not* okay.

5. I'll know for certain I'm exactly
   like Dad.

Foiled Again

Coach emails the team parents:
*It's short notice, but
good news!*

Turns out
we've got ice time tonight
            and again next week
at an arena across the city.
Coach wants us all
to be there.

Oma drops me off a little early
so she can make it to book club
on time. As she drives away
I turn toward the main door.

My feet
transform into
lead weights.

I should go in
            get out of the wind
but I'm stuck
            stalled
in the middle of the sidewalk.

My mouth goes dry
— something's wrong
got to be wrong
but what?

Al's quiet for a change
but I picture him sitting
up there in my brain
            grim expression
and a sad shake of his head
that says he's got a
baaad feeling about
tonight.

            Ignore him, Jonah.

It's just a practice.
It's just

                        hockey
            but lacing up now
            will make the playoffs seem
            all too close
                        all too real

and even though we've
played here before, this isn't
our home arena
not the place I know

inside out.

Will I know
where to go?

Al starts up a movie
in my mind —

> me, stumbling into the
> girls' dressing room
> by mistake

> me, wandering through
> long unfamiliar hallways
> until I'm completely lost

> me, panicking
> but having nowhere
> to run.

I'm probably better off
skipping the whole thing.

I glance over my shoulder
          don't see any of the guys
          from my team
take a right

and duck around the side
of the building.

A man's voice ahead — *Jonah.*
Wrong way, buddy.

It's Coach.

The Usual

I can't shake the feeling
that something's bound to
go wrong
but practice proceeds
as usual
       drills and skills
Rob working with me and Kyle
on stick saves and tracking rebounds.

It isn't until Coach gathers us
for a final pep talk
       focusing
       on the playoffs
that I can't stand still
       breathe too quickly
feel my pulse pounding
in my ears.

Why is my heart beating so fast?
Is it out of   control?
What if it does the same thing
Ty's did and simply

      stops?

I fight to open the gate
need to get off the ice
can't find the latch.

   Rob's hand settles firmly
on mine, stops me
from rattling the gate.

I look at him, silently begging
    just let me out, let me go
and Rob must see it on my face
because he reaches back
opens the gate
without a word.

I find the dressing room
fling down my equipment
sink onto a bench.

I glance around the silent
room — hockey bags, boots
and coats scattered about
cinder-block walls
closing me in.

This is worse.

If my heart
is about to stop
I probably shouldn't be
sitting here
alone.

Number One Reason to Signal for the Trainer

I
can't
do
this
on
my
own.

After My Heart Slows Down

I undo my pads, kick
them aside, pull off my jersey
and stuff it in my bag
          and Al decides
to rewind
          replay
                    tie me up
inside. I head into a stall
disappear behind the metal door
right before the rest of the team
piles into the dressing room.

I lean against the stall wall
close my eyes
breathe
as their voices intrude.

Cole:
*Lay off him, Bennett. We all have
bad days.*

Bennett:
*Yeah, but Vanderbeek's bad days are epic.
I don't know why Coach doesn't
cut him from the team.*

Neither do I, Bennett.
Neither do I.

S.O.S.

Next day after school
I linger at my locker, rearrange
papers and straighten books
while kids push and joke
and locker doors crash
behind me.

When the chaos settles
I head down the long hallway
toward the admin section, slip
through the open door.

The secretary
doesn't look up
from her computer.

Okay, I say, the sound
barely above a whisper.

She types a little more
before turning toward me.

Okay what? she says.

My tongue is dry
as a desert, and my voice
has abandoned me.

I lick my lips
clear my throat
glance over my shoulder.
No one's paying any mind
to me.

I turn back.
Dig around
for a shot
of courage.

The school counselor, I say.
Could I maybe
uh
talk to her
       sometime?

My nose prickles.

Of course, she says
as if it's not a gigantic deal
to see a counselor.

She slides an appointment book

toward her, skims the page.
Ms. Rogers can see you
at 9:40 tomorrow.

That soon?

I take a deep breath
as she scrawls the date and time
on a slip of paper that will double
as a hall pass. I tuck it
in my pocket.

As I shrug into my backpack
and head for the bus
I'm not sure
if I feel better
or worse

but

I did it
   sent up
   my S.O.S.

signaled for the trainer

        myself.

Picnic

I toss my backpack
on the couch, head
for the kitchen and the blue tin
Oma left for us
filled with her homemade
waffle cookies — half of them
thin and flat
            the way Dad likes them
the other half rolled
into crispy tubes. I snatch
a couple of the rolled-up ones
to munch while I do my homework.

When it's almost time
for Dad to get home
I go back to the kitchen
open the pantry cupboard
move to the fridge and stare
inside, searching
for supper. Dad seriously needs
to go grocery shopping.

            He'd go sooner, I'm sure
                  and more often
            if there weren't so many
            decisions involved in

on the table with
the last of the bread.

Dad smiles. *Thanks,* he says.
*Your mom's favorite lunch
— remember?*

As we eat, he tells me
a Before story
of a bread-and-cheese picnic
in the riverside park
the air so thick with mosquitoes
you had to be careful
not to inhale them.

A local news crew noticed us
came by to talk, couldn't believe
we were picnicking
with the bugs.

That night, there we were
on the six o'clock broadcast
Mom smiling out from the TV
swatting mosquitoes as she
laughed about finding
the humor in things
and being grateful for moments
we'll never forget.

Shift

Sometimes
when I think about Mom
I can't sleep, but other times
  like last night
remembering her
helps me sleep better.
I'm glad for the decent rest
but it means I'm almost late
by the time I head outside
to catch the bus.

Rose steps out her front door
at the same moment.
I'm about to wave
but Rose's mom follows
her out. She wraps Rose
in a long hug, too long
for a regular goodbye,
and I look away
a vague melancholy
pinching my heart.

I cross the road. The bus
comes around the corner
and Rose dashes
to join me.

*We're cutting it close
today,* I say.

She doesn't smile
doesn't say anything
even after we've boarded
the bus and claimed a seat.

Rose — I want to ask
if she's okay
but just then the bus bumps
through a pothole
and I drop my words.
I'm about to begin again
when Rose speaks.

She hung up on me.

What? Who did?

Rose takes a deep breath
and then words pour out
in a voice I need
to lean close
to hear.

When I called her — I had
one of her favorite songs
in mind, but when she came
on the line and I said
it was me, she was like
Who? and I told her again
but she hung up. She didn't know
who I was, Jonah.
She didn't remember
her own granddaughter.

A stone lands in my gut.
I can't imagine Oma
not knowing
who I am.

A tear slides down Rose's face
and I become acutely aware
of the space between us
and how awkward
my limbs are. My arm
comes up, my hand pats Rose
on the back, stops
and hovers — what am I
doing? Patting her back
like she's a dog, or a baby
that needs to burp?

Thanks, Rose says
and I realize my hand
has settled on her shoulder.

Stuck

Halfway through silent reading time
my phone vibrates with a reminder:
it's time.

I close my book, pull the crumpled
hall pass from my pocket
but find I'm glued
to my seat.

Can anyone else hear my heart
pounding? I glance around the class.
Everyone has their nose
in a book, but Rose
hums a few notes
without looking up.

I unstick myself, slide
from my seat, barely breathe
as Mrs. Darroch skims
the paper. She nods, and I
slip from the classroom
and into the hall.

Around the corner
I stop.

Long Walk

The alien whispers, hissing
reminders, hurling memories.
I hate this hall, hate the tile,
hate the room at the very end.

I whisper too. Not to Al, but to
the cinder-block walls like the
silent pregame pep talks I give
to my goalposts, making sure
they are both on my side.

*You guys stand strong, don't
close in, hold back the rush
of reasons for me to turn
and run the other way and I
will keep putting one foot in
front of the other. Keep going
keep going keep going.*

It seems to take forever to get
to Ms. Rogers' office but by
the time I knock, Al is quiet.

Fracture

Last time I was here
my whole life fractured into
Before and After.

The Accident

The day of the accident
Ms. Rogers came to my class
pulled me out right in the middle
of a spelling test
steered me down the hall to her office
hand on my shoulder
the whole way
like she was afraid
          she'd lose me.
Oma was waiting for us
and I knew then
whatever had happened
was *bad*.

I remember not breathing
remember the air refusing
to fill my lungs
the room trying to close in
          (exactly the same
          as the night at the arena).

Oma's jaw was set, eyes narrowed
like she was too stubborn to cry
pretending to be strong
or maybe
she really was that strong

— turns out, she had strength enough
to keep the walls from rushing in
and crushing me
when I heard the news.

A delivery truck
traveling fast
had hit the passenger side
of our car. Dad
          in the driver's seat
was banged up
would be okay
but my mom —

the one person who knew
          always
how to make everything okay

— was gone.

I was out of Ms. Rogers' office
through the school door
well on my way to somewhere
by the time Oma caught up to me
in her car.

After

They wanted me to talk to Ms. Rogers
after it happened
appointments every week
but why would I want
to talk about the worst day
of my life? No way
was I going to do that.

No. Way.

We managed
        Dad and I
with Oma holding us together
like glue dabbed on the pieces
of my broken lamp.

But after all this time
        two years
        and four months
        to be exact
so much has happened
so much I can't
        handle
and I wonder if Rose is right
— if talking
might give me more room

to breathe
might open up space
to let in some
light.

Defenseless

Ms. Rogers has a gentle voice
and lines near her eyes
that suggest she's spent
a whole lot of time smiling.

When I step into her office
she rolls back from her desk
swivels to face me, gestures
toward an upholstered chair.

I don't say much
even when she nudges
with soft-spoken questions.
I try, but it feels
like I'm making things worse
like I'm sending away
my defense players
so the opposing team
has open ice, not a thing
between them
and me.

Ms. Rogers sets up
another appointment
before I leave.

Help

Oma picks me up after school
to help move some boxes
in her garage, because her back
is giving her trouble.
When Rose hears why
I'm going, she volunteers
to help. It's not a big job
but Oma seems delighted
with the extra company.

Rose and I finish up
in the garage, then traipse
to the kitchen. It smells
amazing
            buttery and sweet.

Oma's seated by the table
sipping coffee. *Good timing*
she says. *The boterkoek is
almost ready.*

Butter cake, I tell Rose.
*It's so good! Sweet
and almond-y.*

She whispers back

As good as cassava cake?
and winks.

Behind Oma's back
I alternate my hands up
and down, like I'm weighing
the choices, can't decide
which is better.

Rose and I pull out chairs, sit down
too warm from working
to stay in the kitchen
but not about to leave now.

Rose glances around the room
humming a simple melody.
The notes climb up
then
     go
           back
                down
in a rhythm that reminds me
of almost-perfect Saturdays
with my dad.

Oma smiles, then joins in
humming along with Rose
until the cat leaps up

lands softly
on the kitchen table.

Amelia Pond, Oma says
scooping up the ginger cat.
*I don't need your hair
in my coffee, thank you.*

She nuzzles Amelia before
setting her on the floor
then turns her attention
back to Rose.

That's an old song, Oma says.

*One of my lola's favorites.
It's the one I was going to
sing for her today*, Rose says
            a catch
            in her voice.

Her eyes fill
as she chokes out the story
of this morning's phone call.

Oma wraps an arm around
Rose's shoulders, and for a minute
the only sound in the kitchen

is Rose's sniffling, until
the oven timer goes off
with a sharp series of beeps
startling us all
into laughter.

Oma jumps up, grabs
oven mitts, and Rose
            still chuckling
wipes away tears with her sleeve.

*It's usually me that needs
cheering up,* I say.

*We all need help
sometimes,* Oma says
pulling out two round pans
of golden boterkoek.
*Some days we can be
the helper ...*

Like Oma taking care of us
with meals and driving.

Like me skimming the news
keeping the worst stories
from Dad.

And like Rose
singing for her grandmother
and being a friend
when I need one most.

The oven offers a final
high-pitched beep as Oma
turns it off.

Other days, she says
rubbing her lower back
*we need to let the helpers
help us.*

There are a lot of helpers
            come to think of it
— family and friends
but others too, like
Ms. Rogers. My teachers.
Coaches. Paramedics, nurses
and doctors who take care
of people like Ty.
They all help, but I bet
some days they're the ones
who could use a hand.

It's like teamwork, I say
and the thought settles

somewhere deep inside
          brightening
like a torch lit in a dark cave

because teamwork means
even on our worst days
we're not alone.

Ghosted

hey

wanna hang out?

I'm sorry

seriously — really sorry
you have no idea

Alien

My second appointment
with Ms. Rogers, we talk about Ty
and messed-up friendship
and the stress of hockey playoffs
and it's actually
not so bad.
Before I know it
I let down my guard
tell her
            about the alien.

I call him Al, I say
then immediately wish
I'd kept that bit
to myself.

Excellent idea, she says
and I look up to be sure
she's not joking.

I don't know your alien
she says, *but I know others
like him.*

She leans forward a smidge
hands resting loosely
on her lap.

He likes you, she says.

Now she *must* be joking
but she says it again.

He likes you
which is why he sends
all those messages.
He's trying
to keep you safe.

I shift in my seat.
She knows I don't actually
have an alien in my head
                right?

But, she says, *he can get*
carried away, can't he?

No kidding.

I tell him to shut up, I say
but he won't listen.

My words sound whiny
as they escape.

Maybe this week, she says
instead of fighting with him
you could try negotiating.
Tell him he can remind you
about the big stuff
if he leaves
the probably-not-going-to-happen
stuff to you.

I can already see the problem
with this plan: the way Al
tells it, all stuff
is big stuff.

Trapped

Saturday morning
I'm sitting in the kitchen
in my pajamas, eating toast.
Dad brought home a few things
from the corner market
to tide us over, but we still need
to do a major stock-up.

I'm going for groceries
this morning, he says now.
And I have to work this afternoon
so you're pretty much
on your own today, kiddo.

Without hockey
            and without Ty
my Saturday looks bleak.

I could hang out with
the usual group, but all the talk
will be about hockey.

Spending hours ricocheting
between dreams of winning
the championship

      (and feeling guilty

              about wanting to)
and nightmares of all the ways
I'll cause us to lose
is not really my idea
of fun, so when Dad asks
if I want to go with him
to the store, I say yes.

We bus to Save-On-Foods
grab a cart, start on our list.
It isn't long before
we stutter to a stop
midway along the cereal aisle

fenced in
sandwiched

      between rows of

      tall shelves
a million products piled high
towering above us

carts clattering

      a squeaky wheel
baby crying nearby
awful piped-in music

      from the local radio station

and people   everywhere
          squeezing
past our cart.

Dad's gaze swings wildly
looking at everything
choosing nothing
and, oddly, reminding me
of *me* on those days when
the packed hallways
at school suddenly seem
          too loud
          too close
          too much.

I scan the mass of boxes
zero in on a familiar one
nab it and drop it in the cart.

I snatch the list, divvy up items
between us, figuring two
will get through
the decision-making
much faster than one.

You find the pasta sauce, I say
in the next aisle. *The one*
we usually buy.
I'll get the noodles.

We work through the whole list
this way, and by the time
we're outside waiting for a cab
I'm pretty sure Dad feels
as pleased as I do
about escaping unscathed
from the grocery store.

I wonder what would've
happened if I'd stayed home.

Help: Monday Poems by Jonah Vanderbeek

The Save-On-Foods is
an anxiety attack
waiting to happen.

*

Aisles of decisions
shelves of possibilities
overwhelm my dad.

*

I don't mind helping
but someday it would be nice
if Dad could help *me*.

I Can't Hand That In

I'll have to come up with some new
haiku, some Monday Poems
that aren't so
true.

Poetry

Why does poetry
insist on revealing truth
wrapped in syllables?

Focus

Last thing on Monday, I meet
with Ms. Rogers again.
We talk about the noise
— how crowded it feels
in my head
with Al carrying on
the way he does.

Ms. Rogers listens
and nods, head slightly tilted
to one side, every bit as focused
on me and my words
as I am on the puck
in a close game.

When I tell her
Al doesn't seem open
to negotiating, she offers
a different approach.

When it gets too noisy, she says
try pushing pause.
      Push pause
on the what-ifs
and take a moment

to think about
what is.

What is?

What's happening for real.
Right then — what do you see?
What do you hear? Even
taste, smell, feel … What is?

Okaaay, I say
not at all sure
I get it.

Ms. Rogers opens
her desk drawer
pulls out a flat round stone
          (she keeps rocks
          in her desk?)
draws two lines on the stone
with a gold Sharpie
— a pause button.
She slides it across the desk
to me.

Disappointment

Oma calls to say she's sorry
but she can't drive me
to hockey practice
— her back pain is worse.
She has to skip dance class too
so you know
      it's bad.

I catch a ride with Cole.

Coach goes easy on us
— a scrimmage
instead of drills
which is usually great
      almost as fun
      as pick-up hockey
      on the outdoor rink
but not tonight.

Tonight, my reactions
are off, and I misread the play
more often than I
get it right.

At the end of our ice time
Coach gives us a bunch of

reminders for Friday's game
then Rob waves Kyle and me over
for some last-minute
pointers. As we head
off the ice, something like
disappointment
flits across Rob's face
like a shadow. It settles
        dark
and heavy
inside me — he's right.

My team
deserves better.

I'm last to the dressing room.
As I step inside, the room
quiets, and I'm not sure if it's Al
or if it's for real, but it seems clear
everyone was talking
about me
        my lousy play tonight
        and how they hope
Coach goes with Kyle in goal
for the playoffs.

Back at home, I stow
my gear in the garage

         drop the bag
         prop my stick
                  in the corner.

Why
do I keep
playing?

Tuesday Morning Puddle

Ty isn't on the bus, so when I
arrive in class, I'm surprised
to find him at his usual desk.
He catches my eye
and for half a second
it feels normal, like everything
between us isn't ruined.
But then

                    he looks away
laughs with Cole and Bennett
and the other kids who've
gathered around him.

Heat creeps up my neck
and my face
flames.
I slip into my seat

                    s

                    i

                    n

                    k

as low as I can without
sliding right off my chair.
Please, let me melt
            disappear in a puddle
beneath my desk.

Everyone must've noticed
my best friend
isn't talking to me.

Messages

That afternoon there's a school-wide
assembly. We pile into the gym
claim spots on the bleachers, teachers
with watchful eyes
lining the sides of the room.

Rose is with Alexis and Mina
but she makes space for me
beside her. Ty ends up
almost directly behind Rose.
I resist the urge to turn my head
        stay face-forward
        instead.

When Principal Ewing eyes
the eighth-grade students, looking
for a volunteer
I duck my head, a turtle
pulling into its shell.
Not me
not me
not me
        — seriously

do *not* make me climb
down these bleachers to stand in front

of everyone, all eyes on me.

Al gears up, ready to point out
the million ways I'll
embarrass myself. I fumble
to find the pause button, pull it
from my pocket
rub the smooth surface
and imagine subduing Al
by wrapping him in
copious amounts of
hockey tape.

It might not be the strategy
Ms. Rogers would recommend
but it gives me the pause I need.

The principal picks Harjit
and I pull myself out of my shell.

As Harjit winds his way
between students who tip
one way or the other
on the bleachers, making room,
Rose leans in, nods toward the stone
in my hand. *What's that?*

My heart trips.

Nothing, I say
jamming my hand
          and the stone
into my pocket.

A hint of hurt flashes
across her face
and is gone. She hums
a few notes, barely audible
and I remember
when she told me her truth.

I pull out the stone again
flip it over so the gold
Sharpie lines are faceup
on my palm.

Ms. Rogers gave it to me
I say. *For when my anxiety*
gets bad.

Does it help?

I may not have managed
to focus on *what is*
but maybe just holding
the stone will remind me
that calm is possible. Depending

on the day
that might be enough
to settle my mind, enough
to convince Al to give it a rest
for a while.

Yeah, I say. *I think it does.*

Ty shifts behind me, and the movement
catches my eye. He's staring at me
with a look I can't read.
      Does it mean
he can't believe
I told someone other than him
about my anxiety?

Conflicting messages
tangle together
in my mind.

      Should I not have told her?
But I didn't — she read my poem.
      And why would Ty care anyway?
Is he jealous? Mad?
      Does he still want to be friends?
Does he have something against Rose?
      But he likes Rose.

Does he *not* like
that I'm sitting
so close to her?

Principal Ewing's voice
sneaks into my brain, and I
force myself to focus
up front, where she and Harjit
are unrolling a long banner
s t r e t c h i n g it between them
until the message
unfurls:
>   *Welcome Back, Tyrell!*

Everyone claps, and Ty
stands
>   waves
>   grins.

I tumble the stone
over and over
in my hand.

Crunch

At my locker, minding
my own business, triple-checking
my bag for the needed books
don't see it coming:

> Dylan hits me from behind
> sends me crashing against
> the lockers.

By the time I'm upright again, Dylan
is halfway down the hall
with Bennett
        laughing.

Jerk

Dylan Babinsky has been my nemesis
since the middle of sixth grade
since the day he caught me crying
in the boys' bathroom.

It was my first day back at school
      After.

Root

I'm not the biggest player
on my team, but I'm no shrimp.
Still, a guy can get thrown off balance
easy enough, when he doesn't see the hit
coming. When it's a dirty play.

The thing about dirty plays?
They make a guy's teammates mad.

Dylan's laughter stops
when Cole and Harjit step
into his path.

Bennett drifts from Dylan's side
like he's not sure
where he fits in this scene
like the playbook didn't cover
teammates facing off
against each other.

Some fine
foul
language
flies around the corridor
          finds its way
to Mrs. Darroch's ears.

She appears
by her classroom door.

Ends up, there's no bench-clearing
brawl today, but as I head outside
to catch the bus, one truth
takes root inside me:

my friends
really are on my team

                    and I'm not talking
                    about hockey.

Math Problem

If
one
player
becomes friends
with his teammates, then
that player quits, how many games
will the team play before teammates are no longer friends?

Battles

Next morning
I dash across the road
to the bus stop
head bowed against the rain.
Rose and Ty are both
there waiting.

The silent space
between me and Ty
feels like the Grand
Canyon, and after
an awkward minute
Rose starts humming
loudly

       over the pattering
       rain.
I recognize the song

— *Raindrops*
    keep falling
    on my head

and I chuckle.

Ty must know it too
because he says

Maybe if you chose
a song about sun
we wouldn't be
getting soaked.

Rose stops humming
says with a smirk
I could give it
a shot, but then you'd
probably complain
it's too hot.

Probably, says Ty
tipping his head back
eyes squinting
as the rain splatters
his face.

You know, says Rose
you two have a lot in common.

All along, the main thing
we've shared was hockey.
If we don't have that
what's left?

Same thing must be
running through Ty's mind

because he says
Not anymore.

Rose makes a sharp buzzing sound
like he just got the wrong answer
on a game show. *Sorry,* she says.
Please play again.

I laugh, but Ty's quiet
          waiting
               for her meaning.

Your heart problem, she says.
It's a lot like Jonah's
anxiety.

Now Ty laughs
and I agree the idea
sounds ridiculous.

I'm serious, she says.
Your heart problem is invisible
right? We can't tell by looking
there's something wrong.
          But there is.
And it means there are things
you can and can't do.
It means there are different ways

you need to take care of
yourself. Right?

Ty nods. *Yeah. I guess so.*

She turns her head, now
addressing me. Rain drips
from her hair, runs
down her nose.

Isn't it the same
for you? she says.
Only instead of your heart
it's in your brain — your anxiety.
Invisible
            but real.

I can't imagine people being able
to *see* my anxiety, to hear the battles
that go on in my head. That would be
disastrous, wouldn't it?

Or would it be
a good thing?

If the guys on the team
knew why
I had a hard time

maybe they wouldn't look at me
the way they did
after last practice.

The bus pulls up to the curb
and we pile on
find seats — not together
but at least the canyon
between me and Ty
seems a tiny bit smaller
than before.

For Now

The week sneaks by
days disappearing
      slowly at first
then all at once
like an ice jam on the river
breaking up.

By the time Friday arrives
Ty's still barely speaking to me
still choosing to sit
far from me on the bus
      even though Rose
      leaves the space beside me
      free.
I don't have much chance to
worry about Ty, though, because Cole
corners me before homeroom
talks nonstop hockey
totally wired about tonight's
playoff game.

Nine hours! he tells me later
on our way to math
near giddy
with excitement.
Then *seven hours!*

at lunch break.

As Cole counts down
        Al revs up
and when I arrive
at Ms. Rogers' office after lunch
I'm wound tight.

I perch on the chair
shift
        shift again
stand up, whole body
buzzing.

Ms. Rogers waits
        — how odd I must look
        standing here, hands
        twitching, feet shifting.
Finally my head clears a little
and I settle
in my seat.

During our first appointment
I told Ms. Rogers
no way
did I want her
to call my dad. She agreed
but added *for now.*

I guess *for now*
just ran out.

You need to talk to your dad
she says. *Let him know*
you're struggling.

My throat tightens.
You don't understand
about my d — The words
stumble and stall.

If she finds out
how bad
Dad's anxiety is …

She smiles patiently.
It's important we include him
so he can support you.
How can I make it easier
for you to talk to him?

I pick at the edge
of my chair
where a brown thread
juts from the fabric
of the seat.

Jonah, she says
and waits
until I stop picking
and look at her.
I can call him
if you want —

No! That would be worse
would make Dad think
it's a much bigger deal
        too big
            for him to handle.
I'll talk to him.

She studies me
probably trying to guess
if I'll actually do it.
I squirm in my seat.

This weekend, she says
and even though her voice
is gentle
there's no doubt
she's dead serious.

Decision

By the time school's out
my chest feels
like Dylan Babinsky
is sitting on it. My body sinks
onto the bus seat
but my mind
                    drifts
bumps against the bus ceiling
hovers above me, watching
as I lean to the side, let my head
thunk lightly
against the window.

I close my eyes.

As the bus pulls away from school
someone plunks down
beside me. I jolt upright.

It's Ty.

He faces forward, doesn't say
anything, so I keep quiet
glance at him from the corner
of my eye — why
now? Does this mean

we're still friends? Does it mean
he forgives me
for running away
                    or for still being able
                    to play hockey?

After a while, I settle back
            against the seat
watch out the side window
as the world slides by.

We're almost at our stop
when Ty nudges me
with his elbow.
Want to come over tonight?
Maybe watch a movie?

Tonight.

This could be my chance to
get back to normal with Ty.
But the game —

            I could be
a no-show, couldn't I?
They've got Kyle.
Probably no one will even
miss me.

But the pros
don't skip games.
No player would choose movies
over hockey if they're hoping
to make it big — and Ty and I
always imagined
we'd make it. All those hours
on the outdoor rink
practicing
            imitating the pros
dreaming of the day
we'd play alongside
our heroes.

Do I even want that
anymore? And even
if I do, how can I keep
chasing the dream
without Ty?

I take a deep breath
and give him my answer:

A movie sounds good.

Empty

The weight on my chest
       eases
and the tension
in my gut
       unravels
            threads spiraling up
drifting out from
       my shoulders
           arms
               fingers.

Al likes movies — he's quiet
while I escape into stories
       two hours at a time.
A movie will be so much easier
than a playoff game.

A pang of sadness
       sharp
and hollow
rings through me
like a puck shot hard against
the boards
       echoing
in an empty arena.

Am I ready to scrap
the whole anxiety-causing
big-stress, big-league
hockey dream?

Not
        quite.

I rub my palms
on my pants, ignore
the warning siren winding up
in my brain.

Actually, I say, *I can't.*
There's a game. Playoffs.

I shrug and hope
        desperately
that Ty can tell I'm so sorry
for choosing hockey.

Oh, he says. *Right.*

His expression changes
and it feels like a door closing.

No-Win Situation

I miss
the Friday nights
I never had to choose
between friendship and big-league dreams.
Simple.

Off-Season Friday Night Routine

Half a dozen of us in Cole's basement

hands batting an orange road-hockey ball
between shoes or throw-pillow goalposts

strategically rearranging furniture to hide
new dents in the walls before Cole's mom
came downstairs to break up the game.

Alone

Dad arrives home from the
office only minutes
before Cole and his parents
pull into our driveway.
He gives me a quick hug
wishes me good luck
smiles through the pained look
on his face.

*I wish I could be there
for you,* he says.

I know.

*It just wouldn't end well.
You understand, right?
It's ...* He offers a feeble
shrug. *It's too much.*

It's okay, Dad.

He'd be there if he could
        if things
        were different.
Oma would be there too
but her back won't tolerate

driving, never mind
the arena bleachers.

Mom
was always there
every game
        Before.

Inside me, sorrow explodes
like fireworks
— a sudden shock
and then sparks
        slowly
        settling.
I blink a few times
douse the remnants
        of sadness
grab my bag and
go.

Every now and then

missing her
catches me off guard
sadness rushing through me
triggered by the weirdest things.
It hurts worse than anything

but if it ever stops happening
I'll miss it.

Lost

In the early days
after the accident
Dad would check in with me
make sure I ate something
          even if he didn't
hug me hard
when the missing
got to be too much.

Later, though, he got lost
somewhere in his head
          or his heart
spent hours wandering
from room to room
as if he had a vague hope
he'd find Mom hiding
in plain sight.

I'd been back at school a week
figured I'd start back at hockey too
               — of course I would
but as much as Dad had fretted Before
about the dangers
of the game
it was so much worse After.

It was Oma who finally
convinced him
to let me return to my team.

I was relieved to swap
the heavy mood at home
for the cool air of the arena
was even glad for the familiar stench
of the dressing room.
I felt better, like a tiny piece of
normal still existed

but when I headed out the door
on game days
Dad was tense
        tight-lipped
        and restless
every time.

Elimination Game One: The Stars

Warm-up skate
        confusion
wrong way
too fast
some guy comes out of

       nowhere

plows into me hard
sends me   flying.

I land on my back
spread-eagled
       the wind
knocked out of me

fight

       to

           breathe

then air comes in a rush and I'm
gasping it in I'm fine all fine no
problem here.

I sit up, reach for my blocker
search for my   chill

my focus
                      my readiness
to play —

          I can't
do this, shouldn't
do this, it's a wonder
I didn't hit my head
          concussion
too many of those
and you're never the same
too many and you're
out of the game
for good.
What was I thinking?

Now that I've caught
my breath, seems like I can't get
enough, breathe fast, faster
in   out
in   out   in   out
inoutinoutinout.

Someone skates over
stops
      beside me.
I look up
— Cole
checking on me.
     Hey. You okay?
You dropped
like a rock.

Like a …

The word catches
in my ear
snatches my attention
    a rock
image flashes in my mind
    a stone
    two lines
            pause button

Ms. Rogers telling me
to focus on what is.

    What is?

I can't seem to think
of a single thing that *is*
but the attempt is enough
to get me up, enough
to share a shaky laugh
with Thomas and Nick
who've also arrived
at my side, enough
to register Coach's voice
telling Kyle

       he's starting in net.

Worn

When I get dropped off
after the game, I find Dad
pacing the living room.
He startles
when he sees me, obviously
didn't hear me come in.
Has he been tracking back
and forth on the carpet
the entire time I was at the game?
It's a wonder the carpet's not
worn through.

He pastes on a smile
that falters when he
gets a good look at me.
I smooth out my expression
try to look like I don't have a care
in the world.

He doesn't buy it
because he's my dad
and if there's a hint
something is wrong
        could be wrong
                might be wrong
he will assume

something BIG
has gone horribly
terribly
wrong.

Everything went fine, I say
        quickly
before he falls apart.
*Kyle got to play in net
is all. But we won.*

I don't add
that the win means
we'll play the Kings
tomorrow afternoon.

His wobbly smile quirks up
at one side. Is he always this bad?
Always still such a mess
when I'm at a game?

*Dad, is everything … I mean
are you okay?*

For a second, my mind's back
at the arena, Cole hovering
over me, asking *me*
the same question.

I'm just tired, Dad says.
Long day. He sighs heavily.
*I can't wait to be through
tax season.*

He hooks an arm around
my shoulders
pulls me to him
in a side hug.

I'm just glad you're *okay*
he says.

There's no way I can tell him
how far from okay
I am.

Not tonight.

Question

To quit

      or not
to quit

      that
      is

the question.

Done

I walk to the arena early
on Saturday afternoon, find Coach
standing outside our dressing room
        one arm out
           holding the door open
while he talks to someone
inside. He backs out
letting the door close
behind him.

He smiles when he sees me.

First one here, he says. *Good.*
I've got a surprise for you
— for everyone.

He turns back
to the locker room.

Coach, I say, letting my bag
drop. There's weight
to my voice
and Coach pauses
        door halfway open.

As I lay in bed last night

Al was in fine form
sending my thoughts
one way
             then the other
like a player icing the puck
lobbing it to the far end
only to have it brought right back
so he has to deal with it
again.

             And it started all over
on the walk here.

Now, I ignore
the persistent whisper
inside

             but you love
             hockey

swallow down the last
of my indecision.

I'm think I'm done
I tell Coach, nodding
to myself. *Yeah.*
My nod changes to
a slow shake of my head.

I'm not playing today.
Not playing at all.
        I quit.

Coach's brow furrows
        confusion or concern
then his jaw starts working
like he's chewing on the problem
        figuring how to dial back
        my decision.

I brace myself for
        you've got to finish
        the season
bolster myself against
        the team needs you
but before Coach has a chance
to utter a single
guilt-inducing word
someone yanks back the door
from inside, throwing Coach
        off balance.

It's Ty.

Fizzle

Ty's arm comes up
as if to steady Coach
and he steps forward
plants himself in front of me
eyes shooting death rays
at my head.

Quitting? Ty's voice drips
with bitterness.

I thought you might ... I start
to explain, but my words fizzle out.

Might what? Understand?
Be glad I wasn't playing
now that he can't?

I'm sure
        almost sure
quitting is the right thing
to do — for Dad and
for Ty

and for me.

Fighting to keep my voice
steady, I say, *I thought
you'd be happy.*

He shakes his head
anger and sadness swirled together
in his eyes. *I love hockey
and I hate
that I can't play. And yeah
sometimes I hate that you* can.

>   We were supposed to play
>   together.

I search for words
to make things right
but Ty goes on.

*You can't make me happy
by quitting,* he says, his jaw
tight. *And not by playing, either.
It's not your stinking job
to make me happy.*

He turns to Coach
says, *I can't do this today*
and he storms
away.

Coach doesn't utter a word
just holds open the dressing room door
and waits until I change
my mind, pick up my bag
and step inside.

Elimination Game Two: The Kings

We're holding our own
against the Kings
our defense doing a decent job
of shutting down their forwards.
Cole's stepped up his game
            scored twice so far
helping fill the offensive hole
created by Ty's absence
from the team.

In between waves
of *what-ifs* and worries
while the puck
is in the other end
the pause button pops into
my brain and I try again
to think of what is —

the weight of the stick is
just right in my hand

            the blue surface of the goal crease is
            scuffed with snow

                    the blast of the ref's whistle is
                    sharp in my ears

and I breathe easy for a few seconds
until more *what is* truths
come at me like rapid-fire slapshots
from the blue line
one
after
the
other

— my gut is
tight, my heart is
racing, this strategy is
not working
why
isn't it working
I need it to work
need it to do something
anything!

Then again
I'm not puking
and I'm still in position
in goal, which
to be honest
is not   nothing.

Resume

When I arrive at Ty's house
Lewis is on his way
out the front door.

He's in the family room
Lewis says.

I kick off my shoes
pad down the stairs
toward the sounds
of hockey.

I find Ty focused
on the TV screen
Xbox controller clutched
in his hands.

Hey, I say.

He says nothing
keeps clicking
the controller.

I didn't quit.

I watch the screen as Ty
        playing as Connor McDavid
fires a shot at Carey Price.
McDavid scores, and Ty
pauses the game.

We won, I say. *We play*
for the championship
tomorrow.

He finally looks at me
gives a small nod
before turning back
to the screen
and resuming play.

He shifts
        edges slightly to one side
on the couch.
I'm not sure it's an invitation
but I ignore Al's panicked messages
        — *Abort! Abort!*
and cross the room
settle beside Ty
watch the on-screen action.

Ty pauses the game again
reaches under the front
of the couch, pulls out
another controller
and passes it to me
without a word.

Play resumes.

Clear

When I get home
Dad's in the kitchen
dumping spaghetti
into a pot of boiling water.
I wash my hands
reach for plates and cutlery
to set the table.

How was the game? Dad asks.

I almost quit today.

He stops poking
      at wayward noodles
turns from the stove.
I can practically see on his face
the movie that's playing
in his head right now.

      Eyes flash with panic
but I'm standing here
and clearly haven't suffered
catastrophic injury.
      Brow furrows in confusion
because I've been awfully
determined to play

for years.
       And then a brightening — hope
that maybe I *will* quit
— no more putting myself in
mortal peril
a couple times weekly
all season long.

Finally he finds his voice.
Why?

I can't look at him
for this part
focus instead on straightening
the silverware.

Because some days
anxiety
makes hockey really
hard.

Except for the gentle bubbling
in the spaghetti pot
the kitchen is silent.

When I look at Dad
he's staring toward the ceiling
like he's searching

for some other explanation
some other meaning
            behind my words.
His gaze lands back on me
and it's clear he understands.

It's also clear
the truth has broken
something inside him.

I'm sorry, he says.
I've been … I should've …
I'm so sorry.

Fact is, I tried to hide it
as much as he tried
to ignore it.

It's okay, I say.

No, it's not. His lips press together
disappearing for a moment.
Then a croaky voice: *Is it bad?*

I'm seeing the school counselor
I say. *I think it helps — a bit*
anyway.

Dad stumbles over his words.
Well. Good. That's really —
He swallows hard.
Tries again.
I'm proud of you, Jonah.

Proud? Because I've got no
control over my worries?
Because some days I can't help
letting Al be in charge?
Because I seem to have inherited
the one thing I'm sure
he never wanted to pass down?

He smiles then — a small
tired smile
and gives my shoulder
a squeeze.

*It takes a lot of courage
to admit we need help,* he says.
*Even more
to seek it out.*

For some dumb reason
my eyes fill
and the stupid waterworks
begin — but this time it's not

pent-up stress leaking out

it's relief, and
           I think
love.

Unsung

Next morning   too early
I haul the trash can
to the curb, kick
at a lingering mound
of snow in the yard.
When I turn to head back
into the house, there's Rose
sitting on her front step
next door.

Hey, I say. She looks up,
gives me a little wave
so I wander over.

A plate of toast balances
on her knees. She's not
eating.

It happened again, she says.
      Lola
didn't know me.

Her eyes glisten
      like there are tears
      trapped inside
along with the song

she didn't get to sing
for her lola
                    but also
            like she's caught sight
            of disaster creeping close.

I know those eyes.

When Ty was in the ICU
and I was upset, Rose
said she understood.
Back then, she didn't know
about my anxiety — couldn't
understand about that part.
            But she knew
the fear. Knew the worry
that everything
            might not
be okay.

I can't fix anything for
her lola. But I can
sit with Rose

            so I do.

She passes me
a piece of toast.

We don't need to say
anything.

Cheer

We're dressed and ready
for the championship game
except Bennett in the corner
who's still busy applying
excessive amounts
of sock tape.

Coach moves to the middle
of the room, glances
at the clock.

As if on cue, the door opens
and in walks Ty. For me
it's no surprise this time
but most of the team
don't know he came by
yesterday. They mob him
thrilled to see
their star player
their fallen teammate.

Finally Coach breaks up
the reunion, grinning
like someone just promised him
the Stanley Cup.

He'll be in the stands
Coach says. *Cheering you on.*

Ty leaves the dressing room
and Coach launches
into an amped-up version
of his pregame pep talk.

When he gets to the part
where we gather close
huddle
for the final shot
of motivation
he pulls out the big guns.

*Let's win this one
for Ty,* he says.

The team echoes
            hollering, *For Ty!*
and the resounding cheer
rattles me
shakes loose
the bits of confidence
I'd managed to cobble together.

We head out for warm-ups
        with me
            leading the way.

Ty's waiting
this side of the gate.
When I reach him
he raises a hand
for a fist bump.
I tap it with my glove.

You got this, he says
and his voice
holds not a speck
of uncertainty.

He believes in me.

Final Game: The Bears

We're clustered around the bench
getting final instructions from Coach
when I'm distracted by
movement — Rose, leaning over
the railing behind the bench
signaling me.

Keeping an eye on Coach
I inch closer
          to Rose
until I'm near enough
to hear her.

Your dad, she says
her eyes bright.
He's here.

My head jerks up
so I can scan the bleachers.

In the building, I mean
says Rose. *I saw him*
pacing circles
by the concession stand
when I got here.

Why would he come?
He never comes.
Is something wrong?
Is it Oma?

Everything's fine, Rose says
clearly reading the panic
on my face. *He's here
for your game.*

*Is he coming in
to watch?*

She shakes her head.
I don't think so, she says.
But he's here.

Pressure

Our starting lineup skates
into place, facing the Bears.
I move into position
game face on, but insides
      wound tight
give the goalposts one more tap
      for good measure
breathe
focus
ready for puck-drop.

Cole wins the face-off
but his pass to Nick
goes wild.
Bears get possession
lose it at center
get it back, take a shot
      well wide.
Mad dash behind the net
      puck squirts out the side
picked up, stolen, sent down-ice
          sent
back.

Half the period gets eaten up
by a mess of intercepted

passes and missed
shots, until a rebound
off the boards
finds its way onto Cole's stick
and he dekes around
the Bears' defense, fakes out
the goalie and — yes! It's in!

Our bench erupts
            a blazing burst of joy
and even I feel less wound up
like that goal opened a valve
and released
some of the pressure.

After the next face-off
it's less of a scramble
more of a game
as both sides settle in
for some decent hockey
            everyone fired up
            just enough
            to keep me on my game.

Flash

Three minutes left in
the third period
we're tied at four
— so close to surviving
the whole season
so close to becoming
champions.

Bears get a breakaway
left-winger flying
toward me. My heart
hammers.

In the second it takes their player
to stickhandle the puck
into position, a scene flashes
through my mind: Ty
on the outdoor rink
racing at me with a grin
wicked wrist shot releasing
puck zipping
            toward the open spot
            on my stick side
only now it's the Bears' winger
who fires it.

Energy surging I lunge
      get my leg out
      and down
can almost feel the
winter wind on my face
as the puck strikes my pad
rebounds and slides
out of harm's way
      — *SAVE!*

Intermission

Rob claps me on the back
as I leave the ice at the end
of regulation time.

In the dressing room
the mood
is electric, the team
riding high.

Cole is ecstatic:
*Championship game
going to OT! It doesn't
get better than this!*

Yeah, it's been quite a game
exactly what we'd expected
playing the Bears
but I'm ready
for it to be over. That spark
— that moment when it felt
      like the outdoor rink
      like Ty and pure fun
      like I really *loved* hockey

that's gone.

What even *was* that?

The guys ... they're in this
to win. They want this.
They want it for Ty
and for themselves, too
and so do I, but I'm not sure
I want it enough
          to risk so much.

What if I fail?
What if I lose focus
          fumble an easy save?
Sudden-death overtime
means one mistake
and it's all over.
One mistake
and I let everyone
down.

My stomach winds its way
into a tangled knot
making me wish I had
my pause button
or better yet
a barf bag. I jump up
from the bench, rush
to the bathroom as fast

as all this blasted gear
will let me.

Into the stall
          bend forward
          hang
                    over the bowl
breathing fast.

I *hate* this.

My anxiety is as bad as ever.

After a minute or so
of *not* puking
I emerge from the stall
face myself in the mirror
remind myself again
of my dad.

My dad

          who came to the arena
          even though it would've taken
          everything he had

even though whatever alien
haunts his mind
would've been screaming at him
to stay home and not think
about hockey.

He came.

Knowing Dad's out there
pacing *here* instead of at home
knowing he did the hard thing
and showed up
even if he can't bring himself
to actually watch the game
somehow adjusts the volume
in my brain, muffling
Al's voice.

I think of Rose in the stands
and I imagine this is exactly
how it feels when someone
sings away your fears.

It doesn't fix things.
It doesn't mean my fears
won't be back tomorrow.
But for right now
it helps.

Right Now

Even though the stone
from Ms. Rogers
is at home in my jeans
pocket, I take a minute
and create my own pause.

What is real and true
right now?

My dad is
on my side.

My friends are
cheering for me.

I've made some good saves
kept my team in the game.

We might win tonight
              and we might lose
and either way
I'll be okay.

I'll be okay.

Overtime

Al's most quiet when
I'm most focused
and for three minutes and
twenty-nine seconds
the Bears' offense makes sure
I'm super-focused.

They're in control from
the moment the puck drops
don't let off the pressure
for an instant.
Even when we get possession
they break up the play
make sure the game stays
in our end.

One of their forwards
small but super-fast
receives a pass, speeds
behind the net, comes in
for a quick
wraparound shot.
I fling myself
toward the post
try to close
the gap.

The puck
tucks in
between pad and pipe
        slides
over the line

        goal light
        glares red.

Goal

Sudden-death overtime
means our championship hopes
are dead.

Replay

Random gear litters
the dressing room floor
and the stink
          of sweaty gloves
          discarded skates
permeates the room.

My teammates slump
on the bench, heads in hands
because even though we made it
all the way
to the championship game
our season ended
                    with a loss.

It's silent except
for an occasional sniffle
from one guy trying to hide
that he's crying.
Not much point in hiding it
because truth is, we all feel
the same.

A million thoughts mix
in my mind
— not messages from Al

just my own
conflicting
feelings.

       I wish we could've won it
       for Ty.

              I'm glad it's over.

       I *hate* that I let in
       that last goal.

              But it wasn't anxiety
              that beat me.

The door bursts open
and Ty
       strides in
radiating excitement.

What a game! So awesome
but man, I wanted to be out there!

He finds Cole, launches
into an excited replay
of Cole's first-period goal
then turns to Nick

346

recounts his two goals
reenacting the sweet backhander
with surprising authenticity
considering he's in the locker room
with no stick in his hands.

The mood in the room
shifts, brightening as Ty raves
about our defensive efforts, says
Thomas and Harjit were brilliant
and even finds something good
to say about Bennett
      who spent more time
      in the penalty box
      than he did on-ice.
Then he's back to Cole
who scored the tying goal.

Finally Ty drops down beside me
on the bench
goes through save after save
with as much detail and enthusiasm
as an NHL commentator.

And their overtime goal? he says.
You read that guy
like a book — knew exactly
what he was up to.

Darn near stopped him, too.

He slings an arm
over my shoulder.

We didn't win
the league championship
          won't get our name
          on the trophy
          in the glass case
and a big part of me is
weighed down
with disappointment
but another part
          small
          but there
feels like I haven't lost
a thing.

Thanks

When I find Dad
by the concession stand
he's hunched over
       in a hard plastic chair
massaging the back of his neck.
He doesn't straighten up
       until I'm standing in front of him.

We look at each other
without speaking
— me, knowing how hard
       this was for him
and him, I think, knowing how much
       I needed it.

He drags himself up
off the chair.
I let my hockey bag
thunk to the floor, my stick
clatter down beside it
and I wrap my arms
around my dad.

A-Okay

A couple of the guys arrive
in the concession area
and soon Ty and the rest
of the team
appear in a blizzard
of sound and movement
        joking
        and jostling.
I let myself get caught up
in the storm for a bit
then ease out of the crowd.

Come on, says Cole. *We're going
for pizza.*

Nah, I say. *You guys go
without me.*

Aw, come on, Cole says
but when I shake my head
he gives me a look that says
it's okay
        do what you gotta do
then he smirks. *All the more
pizza for me.*

After a raucous round
of fist bumps and back slaps
and more than a few shouts
of *good game, Jonah!*
they leave in a whirlwind
whooshing
toward the exit.

Home

*You sure
you don't want to go out
with the team?* Dad asks.

Part of me wants to be
              with my team
thinks I *should* be
              with my team
but the game
              and overtime
                        and Ty
                                  and Dad
is a *lot* for one day.

I picture Rose
leaning over the railing
to tell me Dad was here
and my thoughts
wander back
to another day
to Rose's song, and a reminder
that sometimes we need help
              and sometimes
we're the helper.

              Can both things be true

at the same time?

Help
        and be helped?

Because right now
I want to help myself
        by saying *no*
        by going home when I need
                to go home
        by not intentionally
                aggravating Al.

You know how you feel
after a day of seeing clients?

He nods.

Going for pizza now
would be like you finishing work
then agreeing to see
another whole batch
of clients.

I don't need to explain
any more than that.

Dad reaches for my hockey bag
I grab my stick
and we head down the
wide hallway
            past the trophy case
push open the glass doors
of the main entrance
and walk home.

Strong

It's been almost a week
since the championship game
and now, on the first day of
spring break, there's little to do
outside. It's a weird
in-between time of year
the ice useless
           but not quite gone
soccer fields still half-buried
           in snow.

Ty and I sit balanced on the boards
of the outdoor rink, legs dangling
against the wood.

I'm still going to skate, Ty says.
Soon as the rink's ready in the fall.

You're allowed to do that? I ask.

Knowing Ty, he'll push
his limits. My mind flashes forward
sees Ty whipping around the ice
his heart stopping
everything happening
           all over again.

Don't worry, he says. *I'll go slow.*
He pats his chest where the
defibrillator hides
beneath his skin. *The last thing
I want to do
is test out this zapper.*

He glances at me, then seems
to find the ground in front of us
quite interesting.

So… he says, nodding
all casual-like.
          His heels thump
          against the boards.
*Are you going out for
the rep team?*

Yeah, I say, even though Al
makes sure to remind me
this could be tough for Ty
to hear. *Coach figures I've got
a good shot at making it
— as long as I don't puke
during tryouts.*

Ty laughs.

I'm serious! If I can't handle
the pressure, they won't want me.
And truth? I don't want
to be the weak link.

You're kidding, right? His brows
pinch together. *Jonah,*
you're stronger than any
of the other guys on our team.
Stronger than I'll ever be.

That can't be true
— don't know why he said it
but my face warms, and a prickly
sensation runs through me.
I laugh to shake it off.

We're both quiet for a minute
until finally I break
the silence.

I'm sorry I let in that goal.
You know — on the night …

The night when everything
went wrong.

Ty says, *I'm more sorry*

I blamed you for it.

Yeah? I say, giving him
a sidelong look. *Well, I'm even sorrier
for starting the fight.*

He smirks. *No,* I'm *sorrier
I had to come rescue you.*

I so didn't need rescuing.

Did too.

Did not.

He hops down
from the boards, but I stay
where I am, glance
over my shoulder
at the remnants of the rink.
All joking vanishes
from my voice.

*I'm sorry I want to keep
playing hockey.*

Slowly, I turn back to face Ty.

He's looking at me
       steady
       and serious.

I hope you make it, he says.
All the way, if that's
what you want.

Celebrate

Oma moves carefully
keeping the position
of her back just so.
She was determined to cook
a celebratory dinner, even though
I told her it wasn't necessary
even though I told her
we'd lost the final game.

Now that we've eaten
Oma shoos us
into her living room, brings out
a tray of oliebollen.
Dad's face lights up
because he loves these
— we both do, but Oma
usually only makes them
for New Year's.
I bite into one of the
deep-fried balls, powdered
sugar falling into my lap.

These are so good, I say.
*Thank you. But we're not
meant to be celebrating.
I told you, we lost.*

Did you show up?
she asks. *Did you try?*

I nod.

Well then, she says.
That's worth celebrating.

Absolutely, says Dad.
I'm so proud of you, Jonah.

What if I'd quit?
Or what if I showed up
but my anxiety
showed up too
and things got
out of hand
⠀⠀⠀⠀⠀and I ran
— what then?
What about those times
when I want to show up
but I simply⠀⠀⠀⠀⠀⠀can't?

My thoughts must be written
on my face, because Oma
inclines her head toward me.

There's a lot to be said

for doing the best you can
with what you have
on any given day.
Some days, that'll be more.
Some days, less.
And that's okay.

Her gaze darts to my dad
before landing back
on me. Dad's not looking
at Oma, didn't catch her
glance, but he nods
in agreement
with her words.

These call for coffee
he says, snitching another
oliebollen from the tray.
Mind if I … He gestures
toward the kitchen.

Please do, says Oma.

She watches him leave
the room, her soft smile
whispering how much
she loves him.

Courage

While Dad clatters about
in the kitchen, Oma offers me
more dessert.

So tell me about the game
she says, setting down the tray.
Not the score — I know
that part.

Dad being there was
amazing. I intend
to say more
but can only stare
at the specks of icing sugar
scattered on my lap. I stuff
my mouth with a large bite
of oliebollen.

After swallowing, I say
It was weird without Ty.
He was there, though
— came to cheer us on.
And there was a moment …

How do I explain that flash
of pure happiness, that memory

of Ty on the outdoor rink
that seemed so real.
I never told Ty
about that, but I suspect
it wouldn't surprise him.
It almost felt like a gift
— from Ty, or from
the hockey gods — reminding
me how much I love
the game, telling me it's possible
I'll love it that much
all the time
                    some day.

In the kitchen, water gurgles
into the coffee pot. My thoughts
drift from the game
            to yesterday
at the outdoor rink.

It's strange, I say.
*Ty told me I'm stronger
than he is. But he's always
been bigger and tougher
— probably always will be
even with his heart.*

There's more than one sort

of strength, Oma says.
I've watched enough hockey
to know that every game
players lace up their skates
go out there, play hard and
give it all they've got. And you
do the same, don't you?
       Every single game. Only
you do it with anxiety.
You do it
while an invisible battle
rages in your head.
That takes courage.
It takes
       strength.

I need a minute
to soak up her words.
She's partly right
       but there's more to it.

Doing the hard thing
does takes strength
but asking for help
when we *can't* do things
       when it all seems
       impossible
that takes strength, too.

I'm glad my dad asked
for help again — he has an appointment
with his doctor next week.
One thing I'm realizing
is how strong
my dad is. I don't think
I would've known that
if I'd never had to ask
for help myself.

Every day, all around me
people do amazing
ordinary things
— making it look easy
or stumbling
or sometimes not managing
        to try at all
and who knows how much
courage
it all takes — doing
or not doing
        trying
        succeeding
        failing
everyone summoning up
strength
their own way
every single day.

It's good to realize that
        about others
but now I know
it's important
to see it in myself too.

Team

NHL playoffs start tonight.
Fans are hyped, wild
with excitement.
The announcer proclaims
the names
                bold and drawn out
as players take to the ice
at a run, revved up and ready
living their dream but still
chasing it too, hoping
and working
and playing hard
for the championship
— and maybe
fighting some invisible
battles along the way.

During the first intermission
my phone pings with a text
from Ty.

> you watching the game?

> yeah

> want some company?

Ty arrives in time
for the second period
and we perch on the edge
of the couch, leaning in
to the action, hollering as if
our voices can reach
the players through the screen.

On commercial breaks
I gush about the skill
of my team's goalie
          mentally filing away tips
          things I want to try
and Ty dissects shot technique
and stickhandling skills
of the forwards.

When play resumes
I sneak a look at Ty
relishing how *right*
it seems, watching hockey
with him beside me.
He catches me looking
          grins
nudges me
with his shoulder.

We both go back

to watching the game
but I can't help thinking
that even without
a cold wind
          on our faces
bumpy ice, wicked
wrist shots and equally
wicked saves

Ty and I
make a pretty great team.

Acknowledgments

I'm so grateful to all who had a hand in bringing Jonah's story into the world. From first draft to published book, there's been a whole team of people with me, playing their positions with skill and kindness and so much heart.

Thank you to my editor, Emma Sakamoto, for her gentle and wise guidance. Thank you to cover artist Julien Castanié and to everyone at Groundwood Books, especially Michael Solomon, Ricky Lima, Nicole Lambe, Fred Horler, Kirsten Brassard, Karen Brochu, Jessey Glibbery, Katherine Kakoutis, Natassja Barry and Christina Valenzuela.

Endless thanks to my kind and brilliant agent, Amy Bishop — best teammate ever! Thanks and love to Kip Wilson, Beth Smith, Carlee Karanovic, Janet Smith, Kristin Butcher, Sheena Gnos, Jocelyn Reekie, Diana Stevan, and Liezl Sullivan — fantastic friends and excellent critique partners. Thank you to Dr. Aadil Dhansay and to Amy LaRocque-Walker for their generous help with my research, and to Nick Green, Tom Green, Jennifer Taylor and Karen Choi for feedback on all things hockey.

Thanks and cheers to the students of Ms. Dent's 2018–2019 grade 4/5 class at Waverley Elementary School, Vancouver, BC, with whom I was paired for the "Kids Need Mentors" program. Their enthusiasm as I wrote this story over the course of our school year together felt like having a great crowd for a home-game.

Thank you to all who respond with kindness when they encounter anxiety in others (or in themselves), recognizing that anxiety is neither weakness nor flaw. Thank you to teachers, librarians and bookish folks everywhere who do so much to get books into kids' hands. And thank you to *you* for reading Jonah's story.

Finally (and especially), thank you to my family for their unwavering love and support. They are my dream team, my all-stars, my top draft picks, always. I love you all!